Praise for *Dear Everybody*

"Kimball creates a sort of curatorial masterpiece, finding the perfect spot for everything that a life comprises… As *Dear Everybody* draws to a close, the letters and accompanying texts become progressively more intense and unexpected… The final power of *Dear Everybody* is that the reader shares in the inevitably conflicted feelings of those closest to Jonathon."
The Believer

"In addition to writing stunning prose, Kimball evocatively hints at entire physical and emotional worlds lying just behind his story's surface. In many cases, the author's verbal compression both amplifies and dampens the tragic clamor of Jonathon's letters… they harbor such a strange emotional power that you'll find them hard to forget."
Time Out New York

"There is a whole life contained in this slim novel, a life as funny and warm and sad and heartbreaking as any other, rendered with honest complexity and freshness by Kimball's sharp writing."
Los Angeles Times

"Quirky, and idiosyncratic, this is a very amusing novel that is oddly endearing, and conceals a warm heart beneath its wit."
Books Quarterly

"In Bender's unsent letters of apology or thanks, Michael Kimball transforms the familiar into the strange ag̲a̲i̲ ̲ ̲ ̲ ̲ ̲ ̲ ̲ ̲ ̲ ̲ est confes-sions are made mome̲n̲t̲ ̲ ̲ ̲ ̲ ̲ ̲ ̲ ̲ ̲ ̲ ̲ ̲ s book."
Chri̲s̲

Praise for Michael Kimball's previous novels

❧

"Not only does he address mortality head-on, but his narrator
describes the deep and powerful love between his grandparents as his grandfather quietly and desperately watches
his wife slowly dying. The grandfather's narration is powerful and
moving... uncomprehending and breathless."
The Observer

"*Highway to the Heart of America*, Kimball's first novel... is
moving and clever: the open road, so long a symbol of freedom
and self-discovery in American fiction, is here rendered as devoid
of promise, embodying desertion, desolation and rootlessness...
Kimball's novel reads as a parable about the death of the family, of
how impossible family life is in a numbedly materialistic society.
However, the largeness of the message should not detract from
the intricacy of fine, precise storytelling... he has taken American
literature somewhere very dark and unsettling."
The Times

"Kimball does have an arresting talent."
Sunday Tribune

"Occasionally a novel by a new writer will cause critics
to choke with excitement. This is one... Kimball resembles
a skinhead at a cocktail party – no quarter given to poxy
commercialism. For that reason alone, his achievement is
admirable. He ignores the media's liaison with trends,
fame, success and trivia."
The Scotsman

DEAR EVERYBODY

ALMA BOOKS LTD
London House
243–253 Lower Mortlake Road
Richmond
Surrey TW9 2LL
United Kingdom
www.almabooks.com

Dear Everybody first published by Alma Books Limited in 2008
This paperback edition first published in 2009
Copyright © Michael Kimball, 2008
Cover Image © Caitlin Hinshelwood
Author Photo © Rachel Bradley

Printed in Great Britain by CPI Cox & Wyman, Reading, Berkshire

ISBN: 978-1-84688-083-4

DEAR EVERYBODY

A Novel Written in the Form of Letters,
Diary Entries, Encyclopedia Entries,
Conversations with Various People, Notes
Sent Home from Teachers, Newspaper
Articles, Psychological Evaluations,
Weather Reports, a Missing Person Flyer,
a Eulogy, a Last Will and Testament,
and Other Fragments, Which Taken
Together Tell the Story of the Short Life
of Jonathon Bender, Weatherman

by

MICHAEL KIMBALL

ALMA BOOKS

Now do you remember?

Jonathon Bender

From the *Jefferson City Chronicle*, January 28, 1999

Local Weatherman Dead, Coroner Rules Suicide

Dan Schneider, Staff Reporter

JEFFERSON CITY – The body of former local weatherman Mr. Jonathon Bender was found yesterday after worried neighbors notified the police that Mr. Bender's car was idling inside his garage. The car radio was still playing.

The report from the coroner's office rules the cause of death a suicide. Mr. Bender left what police are calling a suicide note, though it appears to be a series of letters to many of the people he knew throughout his life. The Police Department says that none of the letters give an explicit explanation for the suicide.

Mr. Bender is remembered for his weather broadcasts on WEXJ, especially his work during the devastating tornado of April 2, 1997 that destroyed much of Market Street and Lime Kiln Road. He was last seen on the air later in that same year. The station did not return calls for comment.

Mr. Bender is survived by his father, Thomas Bender; his mother, Alice Winters (Bender); and his brother Robert Bender – all of Lansing, Michigan. He is also survived by his ex-wife, Sara Olson (Bender) of Jefferson City, Missouri. As of press time, there was no information concerning funeral services.

Everything in Pieces

I never liked my brother much growing up, but I didn't know him well before he died. He moved out of the house when I was still in high school and I never saw him much after that. And it wasn't long after that that our parents separated and then divorced. Our family moved away from each other in different directions and in different ways. I didn't even go to Jonathon's wedding and I never met his wife Sara until his funeral, by which time she was his ex-wife.

We grew up as brothers in the same family, but we had different childhoods. I didn't recognize my mother and father when I read Jonathon's letters. Jonathon's version may have been true for him, but I was the favorite and I don't remember it like that. I don't remember any of the things that Jonathon says our father did to him. I never saw those things happen and it never happened to me. I just thought that Jonathon and our father didn't like each other.

Being Jonathon's younger brother was never easy for me. Jonathon sometimes behaved strangely and he never had a lot of friends. He didn't do well in school or at home. There was trouble in both places for him. He would get detention and get suspended for fighting and skipping classes. Often, Jonathon and our father would get into their own fights after this. I knew that he stopped going to school for a while, but I didn't know that he saw a therapist or that he had to take medication. I just remember that Jonathon was sad and that I didn't want to be around him or admit to my friends that he was my brother.

I don't think that Jonathon would have told me about any of it, though. We didn't talk much when we were kids, and we almost never talked after we became adults. He never told me, for instance, that he and Sara had divorced. I don't know why, but somehow I thought that he had become happy after leaving home.

It was our mother who called me to say that Jonathon had died, and I thought that he must have been struck by lightning when he was chasing a thunderstorm or that maybe he got too close to a tornado. Jonathon was obsessed by the weather when we were kids, and he once told me that the clouds were his friends and that they had formed to protect him from the sun, which he thought was trying to cook him for dinner. He often talked about the weather trying to kill him, but I never thought it would lead to Jonathon killing himself.

My father wouldn't go to Jonathon's funeral, and I didn't want to go either, but I drove my mother down to Missouri for it. After we buried him, we stayed to sort through his belongings. We gave some of his furniture away to Goodwill and then we rented a dumpster to throw almost everything else of his away. His house was filled with so many things that nobody else would want.

But I saved all of the short letters that Jonathon had written in the last days of his life. I also saved a box filled with things that Jonathon had saved from his own life – old family photographs, crayon drawings, yellowed newspaper clippings, pages that were torn out of an encyclopedia, report cards, notes that his teachers sent home, a story he wrote about a summer vacation that our family never took, X-rays from his dentist, his birth certificate, his marriage certificate, his divorce papers – nearly any written document.

The letters are written to nearly everybody Jonathon ever knew. But I don't know why he wrote to the Easter Bunny, to Santa Claus, to our high school, or to a few people who he knew were dead. I don't know why there are so many short letters to so many different people. I don't know why there wasn't just one suicide letter to everybody and I don't know why he never sent the letters either.

I read all of the letters, but I still didn't understand what had happened to Jonathon. That's why I began asking other people about Jonathon's life – my mother, my father, his exwife, anybody I could find who Jonathon named in the letters. I went back home to our old neighborhood and asked some of the neighbors about Jonathon. I talked to the people he went to school with and worked with. I was trying to make some kind of sense out of Jonathon's life, but I didn't believe most of what these other people told me.

My mother didn't want to talk about Jonathon, but she let me read over thirty years of her diaries. She said that most of what I wanted to know would be in them, and I have included many excerpts from them here even though many of the entries seemed doubtful to me.

I also got in touch with Jonathon's ex-wife, Sara, who seemed to resent the fact that I was giving Jonathon so much attention now when I had given him so little while he was alive. She allowed me, though, to include excerpts from the eulogy that she gave at Jonathon's funeral.

Still, it wasn't until I started to ask my father questions about Jonathon that I began to understand his childhood and what my father must have been like for him and also for my mother. I began to realize that I had been wrong about a lot of

5

things concerning Jonathon. You will see what I mean: I have included parts of those conversations here too.

Now I know that Jonathon's life was difficult and painful, and I am ashamed that I did not recognize that fact even though I lived in the same house with him for half of my life. Jonathon's life broke and his mind broke and everything was in pieces. It is all still in pieces. Jonathon left all of these fragments behind and I have tried to put them back together in some kind of order. I hope that this holds him together.

Robert Bender
July 25, 2007
Lansing, Michigan

A Chronology of Jonathon Bender

1966   Conceived, probably on his father's birthday, in San Clemente, California.

1967   Born during The Great Midwest Blizzard in Lansing, Michigan.

1968   Cannot do much for himself.

1969   The birth of his brother, Robert.
Jonathon asks for him to be returned to the hospital.

1970   Fears taking baths.

1971   Fails to blow out the candles on his birthday cake.

1972   Breaks a window with his face.
Thinks he has gone blind.

1973   Falls in love with his babysitter.
Beaten by his father for leaving a door open.

1974   Cannot stop hiccupping.
Runs away from home; returns the same day.

1975   His father teaches him how to fight.
Thinks he is crowned the Burger King.

1976   Wears red, white, and blue clothes every day for a whole summer.

1977   Tries to stop his father from choking his mother.

1978   Runs away from home again and hides from his father
       in the neighbor's garage.
       His blackouts begin.

1979   Thinks cancer is contagious.

1980   Begins high school.
       Worries he caused his grandfather's death.

1981   Finds his father's pornography and begins to learn
       about women.
       Feels he is beginning to rot after getting a cavity filled.

1982   His first visit to a psychiatrist.

1983   His first sexual experience with a girl who is not in a
       magazine.

1984   Loses virginity; does not want it back.

1985   Breaks up with first real girlfriend.
       Graduates from high school.
       Leaves home to begin college.

1986   Tries to hug his father, but his arms are not long
       enough.
       His mother worries about him being away at college.

1987   His parents separate.
       Considers suicide after reading depressing novels.

1988   Stops going to class or studying.
       His parents divorce.
       An airplane explodes over Scotland.

1989   Graduates from college.
        Cuts off contact with his father.

1990   Disappears for a year.

1991   Chases a tornado.
        Lies on resume to get weatherman job.
        Gets camera time in a small market.

1992   Meets Sara Olson, who recognizes him from
        television.

1993   Starts living with Sara.
        Gets distracted by airplanes.

1994   Attempts to make it rain; fails.
        Marries Sara.

1995   Attempts to conceive a child with Sara; fails.
        Buys a house with a cracked foundation.

1996   Committed to a mental hospital by Sara.
        Months pass; gets himself out.

1997   Sara separates from him.

1998   Begins looking for his childhood.
        Loses job.
        Refuses to sign divorce papers.

1999   Tries to remember his whole life.
        Commits suicide in his car in the garage at
        his home in Jefferson City, Missouri.

The Life of Jonathon Bender
(b.1967–d.1999)

1999

Dear Everybody,

Here I am sitting in my kitchen with everybody who I can remember and it is crowded in here. Everything that I can remember is falling out of my head, going down my arm, and out my fingers. I can feel it happening inside me and sometimes it hurts.

The kitchen needs to be remodeled, but Sara and I divorced before we could turn it into something new again. The flowered wallpaper is peeling in places and now I can see all of the cracks in the plaster underneath. Now I can see that the flowered wallpaper was holding the wall both together and upright.

My mom and my dad aren't married anymore either, but they are both here. I think that I see my brother Robert toward the back of the room. I haven't seen him in years, but I don't think that he wants to talk to me. We never knew what to say to each other anyway.

I'm not sure what to say to everybody yet. It feels as if everything is falling down around me. The kitchen floor is old linoleum and I don't know whether the flooring underneath it is any good anymore. Whoever lives here next will probably have to tear it all out.

All four of my grandparents are dead, but they are here too. I have invited everybody.

There is Santa Claus and the Easter Bunny. They really do exist, at least for a little while.

There is my first grade teacher, Mrs. Sussex, and my high school history teacher, Mrs. Thorp. I wonder if they know that I am almost dead.

There are some of the people from the neighborhood where I grew up – Mrs. McCoy, Mr. and Mrs. Evers, Mr. and Mrs. Hall. There are some of my childhood friends. Hi, Steve. Hi, Jim. Hi, Al. I'm glad that you could come.

There is my track coach, Coach Brackett. I recognize him by the stopwatch hanging around his neck. There are some of my other teachers from middle school and high school, and a few of my professors from college. I hope that I remember everybody's name.

Whose dog is that? There is a stray dog in here or maybe it is the one my parents never let me have. There is a brown squirrel in here too and the sun is in here keeping everybody warm.

There are so many things that I already can't remember that it makes me feel as if little pieces of me are already missing.

The countertops are made out of all of these little tiles and some of them are cracked and missing too. The cupboards have so many layers of paint that they either get stuck or they don't close anymore.

Here are my therapists – Dr. Adler and Dr. Morris and Dr. Gregory. It looks as if they brought me some more medication. I tried to keep taking it. I tried to get better.

There is my babysitter Kathy Granger. I wish that my mom and dad could still hire her to watch over me for two dollars an hour.

There are a bunch of my ex-girlfriends here. I can see Candace and Marie and Angela and Megan. I can see the second Megan. I can see Debbie and Laura and Simone and Amanda. I haven't seen any of them for years, but they all look the same age as they were when they liked me or I liked them.

I have disappointed so many people.

There is David Vaughn, my roommate from freshman year of college. Hey, David. He just nodded back to me. He's talking to Carol McAnallan. I'll write about that later.

I'll try to remember everything that I can. The only thing holding me together is my past.

There is Mr. McComb, the news director from WEXJ, the television station where I was the weatherman. Now he knows that I won't be forecasting the weather anymore. There will still be weather. There just won't be me.

I don't see Sara anywhere, though. Maybe she is waiting until later in my life to show up, until I have written to everybody else. I hope so. I hope that I get to see her again.

I'm going to write everybody letters about everything that happened. I always thought that my life had been continuous, but now I can't remember anything except for isolated instances. I hope that these were my defining moments.

> Your son, your grandson, your brother, your friend
> or neighbor, your student or classmate, your patient,
> your co-worker, your ex-boyfriend or ex-husband,
> your ex-everything, the weatherman,

> Jonathon Thomas Bender
> 1947 Riverside Drive
> Jefferson City, Missouri

1966

Dear Mom and Dad,

Do you ever wish that the sperm and the egg that became me wasn't me? I'm sure that you must have been expecting somebody else from all of that pleasure.

From the Diary of Alice Bender
June 7, 1966
Tom was so angry when I told him I was pregnant. He picked up the little alarm clock from the bedside table and threw it against the bedroom wall. Its glass face shattered into little pieces and the clock stopped at that hour and minute. Our lives kept going though. That couldn't stop what had already happened. I'm still going to have a baby.

From a Talk between Robert and Thomas

Tom: I don't know why I believed your mother when she said that she wouldn't get pregnant. It wasn't until her period was two weeks late that I realized that I was going to become a father even though I didn't want to be one yet. I didn't want to buy a crib and a baby stroller, all of those diapers and baby clothes. I had been saving up for this red Corvette and a split-level house.

Rob: You know that Jonathon knew that, right? He knew that you never wanted him. We all did.

Tom: I still blame your mother for all of that. If she wouldn't have gotten pregnant then, if that would have happened later, then we would have had a different child from Jonathon. Or maybe we just would have had you. We never needed both of you.

The Pill (1966–)

The Pill, an oral contraceptive, has been available since 1960 in certain parts of the world, and since 1966 in the **United States of America**, when the **Food and Drug Administration** formally classified it as safe for human consumption. The Pill has become extremely popular and it is widely believed that many children – *including Jonathon Thomas Bender* – would never have been born had The Pill been available earlier. In fact, certain demographers think that the world's population may begin to dwindle with worldwide distribution.

See also Contraception vs. Abortion; Population Control; World Population

[Among all of Jonathon's other papers, there was this page that was torn out of Volume P of *The American Standard Encyclopedia*. These were the encyclopedias that we grew up using for school reports or for when we asked our mom or dad a question that they couldn't answer. The strange thing is that the part in italics was written in by hand. Even stranger, it doesn't appear to be Jonathon's handwriting or my mother's or even my father's. I don't remember doing this, but I'm not sure who else might have done it. (RB)]

From the Diary of Alice Bender
October 7, 1966
Tom and I decided to leave California for Michigan, for the baby, for our family. I want to be surrounded by both of our families when we start our own. I don't think Tom really wants to leave. I've never been a mother before. I'm afraid I won't know how to do it.

Dear Mom and Dad,

I wish that you would have stayed in California after you conceived me. I didn't want to move to Michigan with you. I think that I would have turned out better if I could have eaten more oranges and worn shorts all year round. I think that I might have grown up to be a taller man and maybe had a sunnier disposition.

1967

From the *Greater Lansing Herald*, January 29, 1967

Snow Baby Born at St. Lawrence Hospital

Catherine Mason, Staff Reporter

LANSING – The Great Midwest Blizzard of 1967 could not stop Jonathon Thomas Bender from entering the world on the afternoon of January 28th at 2:23 p.m., but the Bender family almost didn't make it to the hospital in time.

The father, Mr. Thomas Bender, said that Baby Jonathon was already two weeks past due and that he had been shoveling snow off his front walk and his driveway for the last two days of the blizzard. He wanted to be ready when his wife went into labor. Mr. Bender's shoveling had little effect, however, after the blizzard's 50-mph winds blew the 28 inches of snow into 15-foot snowdrifts. The young couple could not back their car out of the driveway and had to wait for the Ingham County Department of Transportation to plow the streets from their house to St. Lawrence hospital.

The new mother, Mrs. Alice Bender, said, "I was afraid I was going to have the baby in a snowdrift. I thought we might have to live in a snow fort or an igloo." The new father shook his head and said, "I'm glad it was a boy."

During the blizzard, 76 people died throughout the Midwest. The mother and child are doing fine.

[This newspaper article was folded up and tucked into our mother's diary. My mother and father must have been excited about making the newspaper. (RB)]

21

Dear Mom and Dad,

I didn't know that I was two weeks late and that you were waiting for me. But it always made me feel special to know that Ingham County had to send a snowplow out to our house. It always made me feel special to think of Dad driving the car so slowly behind the snowplow and Mom with her hands on top of her stomach as if I were an important, but breakable, package. I always thought that there was some important destiny in that for me. I always thought that the path that was cleared through all of that cold and snow was somehow going to determine the rest of my life.

From the Diary of Alice Bender
January 29, 1967
I was too far into my labor when I got to the hospital. They couldn't give me an epidural. Nobody tells you how much childbirth really hurts. I kept passing out. One of the nurses would pinch me on the arm and slap me on the cheek to bring me back. They kept telling me to keep pushing, keep breathing, but I couldn't get Jonathon to come out of me. Then they made me stop. Jonathon wasn't coming out right. The umbilical cord was wrapped around his neck. The doctor had to cut my stomach open so Jonathon didn't kill himself.

Dear Mom,

I don't think that I ever wanted to leave you. I think that I wanted to stay inside of you. I think that I wanted to keep swimming in all of that warm water.

From a Talk between Robert and Thomas

Tom: I didn't want to hold your brother when the nurse handed him to me. He was so small and his skin and his hair were so red. He didn't look anything like me. I didn't really see how he could have been mine.

Rob: Whose son did you think he was?

Tom: He started crying when I held him and his face turned even more red and he balled his little hands up into little fists like he wanted to fight me. Your brother stopped crying when I handed him back to his mother. It turned out that your brother was always like that.

1968

Dear Mom and Dad,

I must have liked the way that you held your arms out to me so that I would walk across the living room to you. I'm pretty sure that I was trying to keep my balance. I don't think that I meant to keep falling down.

Do you remember what it felt like when I made it across the room and you embraced me? I don't. I don't think that I was old enough to remember it.

From the Diary of Alice Bender
September 29, 1968
Jonathon can be such a difficult baby. He is difficult to feed
and difficult to put down to sleep. He won't open his mouth
when I try to feed him. He'll spit the food back out when
I do get a spoonful of it into his mouth. I end up scraping
the food off his chin and the side of his face. I just read in a
parenting book how a baby's temperament usually predicts
his temperament when he is an older child. I hope it isn't
true.

Dear Mom and Dad,

I don't know why I was so sick when I was a baby or why I
cried so much, but I don't think that I ever wanted you to put
me down in my crib. I couldn't get out by myself and I couldn't
tell if you were going to come back for me. I think that I kept
crying so that you wouldn't leave me alone. Could you hear
me?

Can anybody hear me?

From the Diary of Alice Bender
December 16, 1968
Jonathon has been keeping us up at night crying. We aren't getting much sleep. I have tried holding him. Tom has tried too. I have tried reading to him and singing to him, giving him a bottle and giving him a pacifier. I sit up with him all night in his baby room. J only stops crying when he gets so tired that he falls asleep. I'm surprised at how angry T gets with J when he cries. He yells at J as if J can understand him, as if he isn't a baby. I don't know how to make him stop crying, though. I finally took Jonathon to the doctor today. The doctor says it is probably just an ear infection and lots of babies get them. He gave me antibiotic eardrops, but I don't know what I will do if they don't work. I hope there isn't anything else wrong with him.

1969

Dear Mom and Dad,

I wasn't trying to catch the flu bug that they said was going around, but I never saw it or heard it and I didn't smell it or taste it. I don't know how it got inside of me and I didn't realize how much sickness was inside of me either.

From the Diary of Alice Bender
March 15, 1969
Jonathon asked why my stomach keeps getting bigger. I told him there's a new baby inside me. He got upset and told me he is the baby. I had to explain how a family could have more than one baby and how we would never replace him. J doesn't seem to believe me.

From a Talk between Robert and Thomas

Tom: Your mother and I thought that your brother was old enough to sleep in his bed without the safety bars on the side anymore, but one night a loud noise woke me up. I checked all of the windows and doors, and I couldn't find anything wrong until I found your brother in the fetal position on his bedroom floor. He moaned like he was in pain when I picked him up, but he didn't wake up. I put him back in his bed and tucked him in tight so that he wouldn't fall out again. I have always wondered why he didn't wake himself up when he fell out of bed. I think that he must have been good at absorbing pain, even in his sleep.

Dear Dad,

Thank you for taking me to the barbershop to get my hair cut for the first time. I know that it was long and curly and that Mom said that it looked pretty, but I didn't like all of the other moms and dads thinking that I was a girl either.

1970

Dear Mom and Dad,

Here's the reason that I pulled the stitching out of my feather pillow and then pulled all of the feathers out of it too: I thought that I was going to find a bird.

From the *Greater Lansing Herald*, June 1, 1970
Violent Earthquake in Peru Caused by Fault
David Rissman, Newswire

PERU – Yesterday, an earthquake in Peru killed somewhere between fifty thousand and seventy thousand people. The body count continues to be uncertain. It may always be.

Authorities do not know whether they will find everybody under all of that dirt, under all of those rocks, inside of all of those broken and falling down houses. However, geologists have explained the cause of the earthquake: a fault in the earth that had been there for years. The fault only became evident when the surface of the earth started moving so violently.

[It is unclear why this newspaper clipping was among Jonathon's other papers. Jonathon could not read at the time the article is dated and I don't know why my mother or father would have saved it. They could not have known that Jonathon was going to become a weatherman. They could not have known that Jonathon was going to become his own natural disaster. (RB)]

From the Diary of Alice Bender
May 4, 1970
I changed Robert's diaper and then I walked into the
bathroom to wash my hands. I found hair all over the
bathroom floor. I found Jonathon playing with his fire engine
in the backyard. I couldn't believe it when I saw him. His hair
was so chopped up you could see his scalp in some places.
I explained how I had to even it out. He still cried when I
shaved his head. The tears made the hair stick to his face. It
made me cry too. It probably looked like I had to shave his
head because he had lice.

Dear Mom and Dad,

I know that I should have admitted to it when I did it back
in 1970, but it was me who drew on the living room walls with
the crayons. I thought that I could draw a picture of somewhere
else and that I would be able to go through the living room
wall to that place. I didn't realize that what I drew wasn't
real and that crayon drawings can't take you to Grandma and
Grandpa's house or take you to the moon.

From the Diary of Alice Bender
November 29, 1970
I couldn't get Jonathon to take a bath today. I put some bubble bath into the bathwater to make it more fun for him, but he was terrified. Jonathon ran out of the bathroom screaming. I found him under his bed. I pulled him out and calmed him down and asked him what was wrong. He told me the bubbles in the bathtub meant the water was boiling. He was afraid I was going to cook him.

1971

Dear Mom and Dad,

Do you remember how I couldn't blow out the candles on my birthday cake even though there were only four of them? Do you remember how they kept lighting back up no matter how hard I blew on them? I started to cry because I didn't think that I would turn four years old or that we would eat my birthday cake. I didn't understand that the candles were supposed to be a joke.

MICHAEL KIMBALL

Dear Mom,

Thank you for teaching me how to tie my shoes into double knots so that my shoelaces would stop coming untied so much and so that I would stop tripping over them and falling down and skinning my hands up and tearing holes in the knees of my pants and skinning my knees up too. Thank you for putting the pink medicine on my hands and my knees and then also for putting the Band-Aids on them. It was 1971 and those patches that you sewed over the holes in the knees of my pants made me look so cool.

Dear Mom and Dad,

I didn't flush the toilet because I was really excited about it. I dragged you into the bathroom to show it to you because it was so big and I had done it all by myself. I thought that you were going to be proud of me.

From a Talk between Robert and Thomas

Tom: We didn't have enough bedrooms for everybody after you were born and I wanted a bigger house. That's why we bought the place on Harriet Street. You and your brother each got your own bedroom and you got to go to a better school. There was a fourth bedroom because your mother and I had always talked about having another kid. She wanted a girl, but I didn't want to risk having another one like your brother. I eventually turned it into my home office.

Dear Mom and Dad,

I put up such a fuss about moving away from our house on Ionia Street because I thought that you were going to leave me there. You hadn't packed me up inside a cardboard box like you had nearly everything else and I didn't think that you were going to move me with you and all of your other stuff.

From the Diary of Alice Bender
October 19, 1971
Tom got a new job, which means more money and it means he can buy some of the things he has always wanted. It also means he will be gone on business trips nearly every week. The house is bigger, but it is quieter. I am lonely. Jonathon is asleep and Robert is asleep. It's almost winter and it's cold outside. I'm waiting for Tom to call me from his hotel room in a city that is too far away from me. I wish I had somebody to talk to.

Dear Dad,

I always liked it when you brought those tiny soaps and little bottles of shampoo home from your business trips for Robert and me. I always thought that you had gotten them especially for us since they were child-sized.

From a Talk between Robert and Thomas

Tom: I liked going away on business trips. It made me feel important to leave all of you at home and travel for the rest of the week. It made me feel like I was doing important work.

Rob: Didn't you miss us?

Tom: I liked being waited on when I was on airplanes and in restaurants. I liked the room service and the maid service and the turn-down service when I was in hotel rooms. I liked being the person who other people were waiting to meet with in offices all over Michigan and Indiana and Ohio.

From the Diary of Alice Bender

November 12, 1971

I took the kids to the mall today. I didn't have any money to buy anything. I was just walking around. I wanted to be somewhere besides inside the house. I wanted to see people who were older than three years old. I wanted to talk in an adult voice. I was looking in one of the store windows and pointing little things out to Robert. When I looked around I couldn't find Jonathon. Then I saw something splashing in the water fountain in the middle of the mall. I knew it was him. He was picking up the small change that people had thrown in. When I asked him why he was doing it, Jonathon said, "Daddy won't have to go away so much if I give him all of this money."

1972

Dear Mom and Dad,

I woke up screaming that one time because of all that eye
gunk holding my eyelashes and my eyelids together. I couldn't
open my eyes up. I thought that I had gone blind.

From a Talk between Robert and Thomas

Tom: You and your brother used to be so happy when I
       came home from a business trip. Both of you would
       gather around me when I walked in the front door.
       You would follow me into the bedroom and stand
       around me as I unpacked my suitcases. You always
       hoped that I had brought you something back besides
       me. You always wanted souvenirs from places you
       had never been. Do you remember any of this?

Dear Mrs. McCoy,

I'm sorry that I broke the storm window in your back door
with my face. I'm sure that you were a good mom, but I didn't
want to stay with you when my mom left me with you to babysit
me. I knew that my mom was going on her first job interview
since I had been born, but it wasn't until I was standing inside
your yellow kitchen that I realized what it would mean if
she got that job. I couldn't stand the idea of my mom leaving
me with somebody else for most of the week. I could still see
my mom walking down your driveway toward her car, but I
didn't realize that there was that storm window between my
mom and me and that I was just looking through it.

Dear Mom and Dad,

I liked building sand castles and looking for shells and turtles and dead fish on the beach that time that you took us to Lake Michigan. But I kept running away from the blanket that you had laid out on the beach and trying to swim out into the lake because I had noticed that everything got smaller the farther away that it got from us. I was trying to swim out to the horizon where the boats kept disappearing. I wanted to see where everything went when it disappeared.

Dear Grandpa Bender,

Do you remember when you showed me your hand and told me that you had lost one of your fingers? Do you remember how I spent that whole day at your house looking for it for you? I didn't understand why you weren't looking for it too. I didn't realize that it got cut off with a band saw by accident or that that had happened years ago.

From the Diary of Alice Bender
September 5, 1972
This morning, I walked Jonathon to the bus stop. It was his first day of school. He didn't want to go. He just stood next to me, a little behind me. He held onto my leg. He didn't understand why I was making him go. I tried to explain to him that all of the boys and girls his age go to school. But he said he wasn't like the other boys and girls. When the bus came, I had to pick him up, carry him onto the bus, and set him down in a seat. The look on his face when I left him there made me feel sick.

This afternoon, I waited for Jonathon at the bus stop. I looked for his face in the windows of the bus as it pulled up to the bus stop. Jonathon was so surprised when he saw me. He just stared at me with his mouth open. I smiled and waved at him until his face changed into a smile. He ran off the bus, jumped onto the sidewalk and then into my arms. It made me happy to have him with me again. I missed him too.

[When Jonathon first started going to school, I thought he was being punished for something bad he had done, probably because he didn't always finish his dinner. I thought that I got to stay home because my mom liked me better. (RB)]

Dear Mom,

Thank you for walking me to the bus stop for my first day of kindergarten. I liked standing there with you. I liked us standing there with the other moms and their kids. I felt really proud that you were my mom and that I was your son. I wouldn't have known how to go to school without you.

Did you know that they were going to teach us how to take naps and eat snacks? Did you know that they weren't going to let me go home until I drank all of my milk?

I didn't always finish eating my dinner because I didn't think that it was really making me any bigger. I didn't believe you when you said that I needed to eat more bread and meat and potatoes so that something would stick to my ribs. I kept feeling around my ribs and between them, but none of that food seemed to stick to my ribs no matter how much of it I ate. I didn't realize that you were really saying that you needed me to keep eating so that I could grow up to be bigger and stronger than Dad.

1973

Dear Easter Bunny,

My mom and dad got mad at me because I wouldn't stop looking for Easter Eggs around the house and in the backyard, but I thought that you were supposed to come to every kid's house. I was hoping to find those plastic eggs with the candy inside them hidden behind the curtains or in the bushes or in the long grass in the backyard. I thought that there might be jelly beans or marshmallow bunnies or those little chocolate eggs wrapped up in different colored tin foil. You knew that I lived there, right?

Dear Kathy Granger,

Do you remember when I used to stand on the sidewalk outside your house and yell out your name until you came out to play with me? I didn't know that you were just my babysitter and that my mom and dad paid you to watch me. I thought that you really liked me – and not just because I was a cute little boy. I thought that we were going to get married when I was old enough.

From a Talk between Robert and Thomas

Tom: I started to like the quiet of hotel rooms. So when I was home, I didn't really want to play with you or your brother. I really just wanted to sit in a chair on the back porch or sit on the couch in front of the television. But your brother could be relentless. He always wanted to play "catch" or Frisbee or some board game or cards. I would tell him to go play with you, but he would say that you were too little. You probably didn't want to play with him either.

Rob: That's not true.

Tom: Anyway, that was why I taught him how to play solitaire. He was so happy that I was teaching him how to play the game that it made me like your brother even less than I already did.

[My father was right. I didn't like playing with Jonathon either, but I didn't want him to know that. I knew how mean I was to Jonathon, but it made me feel terrible to learn how mean my father was to him too. (RB)]

46

Dear Mom and Dad,

I was just pretending to be asleep in the bed of the station wagon on that drive home from Lake Michigan. I didn't open my eyes up when you shook my shoulder because I wanted one of you to pick me up and carry me into the house and up to bed.

From the Diary of Alice Bender
July 21, 1973
It was hot today and muggy. Everything felt sticky. This morning, J & R were playing the Saturday morning cartoons too loud. That woke Tom up in a bad mood. The kids were laughing and T was yelling. That was how the day started. By afternoon, the day had turned into the kind of hot where you stick to the furniture. J came into the kitchen and asked for something to drink. His father told him he could get it for himself. J did, but he didn't close the door after he got his can of pop out of the refrigerator. T told him to close it. J wouldn't do it. J tried to run out of the kitchen. T grabbed him and stood him in front of the open refrigerator. J still wouldn't close the door. T hit him. T told him again to close it. J still wouldn't do it. T hit him again. I don't know how many times this happened. I realized T wasn't going to stop hitting J and J wasn't going to close the refrigerator door. I made T stop hitting him long enough that J could get away from him – even though I know that it will be me later tonight. At least T leaves on Monday.

From a Talk between Robert and Thomas

Tom: I was away from home so much that you and your brother got used to me not being there. You didn't seem to like it anymore when I came back home. You didn't greet me at the door anymore or even come down from your bedrooms, either of you. You didn't stop watching TV or even stop doing your homework. That's why I used to slap you two on the side of the head. Sometimes, I had to remind you that I was your father.

Rob: I don't remember you ever doing that. Are you talking about the way that you used to mess up our hair? I thought that that was just how fathers showed their affection for their sons.

Dear Tooth Fairy,

I was afraid to pull the loose tooth out of my mouth even though I knew that you would bring me a quarter for it if I left it under my pillow. I wanted the quarter, but I was afraid of the blood and I was afraid that I was going to start losing all of my teeth and that they wouldn't grow back and that I would have to get fake ones like my Grandpa Bender did.

From a Talk between Robert and Mrs. Sussex, Jonathon's
First Grade Teacher

Mrs. S: It was the year that you kids learned how to count
past ten and practiced penmanship and made things
out of construction paper. Jonathon was good at
reading and at math, but he didn't really stay inside
the lines when he colored, which was a big problem
in the first grade. But the thing that I remember most
about your brother was his problems at lunch. Your
mother used to send notes to school explaining that
Jonathon didn't have to eat anything that he didn't
want to, but the lunch ladies still made him stay in
the lunchroom until he finished all of his food. There
were many afternoons when Jonathon didn't come
back from lunch with the other kids in the class.
I would find him sitting in that big cafeteria all by
himself and rescue him from the lunch ladies.

[Mrs. Sussex was old when Jonathon and I were in elementary
school, so I was surprised that she was still alive and that she
remembered so much about one of her students. Jonathon
must have made an impression on her. (RB)]

Dear Mom and Dad,

I know that I must have looked strange after I pulled most of my eyelashes out of my eyelids. It must have looked as if there were something wrong with me. But I want you to know why I did it: this girl at school told me that if you blow on your eyelashes and they fly away it's good luck.

Dear Santa Claus,

Thank you for bringing me the bike with the banana seat for Christmas and for putting training wheels on it so that I didn't fall off it when I rode it. I knew that there was too much snow on the ground for me to ride it outside then, but I was so excited that you knew where I lived and that you thought that I had been a good enough boy to get a bike that I pretended to ride it in the living room. Did you see me? I was turning the handlebars back and forth as if I were going around corners.

Dear Mom and Dad,

Why did you teach me the child's prayer that was about me dying in my sleep before I woke up? I think that that was why I so often dreamed that I was dying, which was why I didn't want to go to bed at my bedtime. It was common knowledge among children then that if you died in your dreams, then you died in your real life too.

1974

Dear Grandma and Grandpa Winters,

Thank you for giving me the Etch-a-Sketch for my seventh birthday. I liked drawing with it better than drawing on the walls, but I always felt sick when I shook it and everything on its magic screen disappeared. It reminded me of how my dad would grab me by both of my shoulders and shake me until everything went blank inside me too.

From the Diary of Alice Bender
April 15, 1974
J's school called me at work today. His class had been on the playground looking at a solar eclipse through a telescope. Jonathon had looked directly into the sun. The school nurse told me J might have damaged his eyesight. I left work and took him to the eye doctor. Luckily, the blindness is only temporary. I am amazed at how many different things can go wrong with the child.

Dear Mom,

Thank you for picking me up from school and taking me to the eye doctor. I liked those big black plastic sunglasses that he gave me to wear. I liked it when you said that they made me look like a movie star.

Dear Robert,

Do you remember when we saw *Planet of the Apes* on television? I remember that I had difficulty separating the apes in the movie from the guerrillas that I would sometimes hear about on the evening news. I knew that we were fighting a war then, but I didn't know that you could spell guerillas that way or that when you did it referred to people. I knew that gorillas were apes, but I didn't know that guerillas and gorillas were different things. I didn't understand why everybody wasn't as afraid as I was.

From the Diary of Alice Bender
May 25, 1974
I felt so bad for Jonathon. I had been standing at the kitchen window watching him play in the backyard. I saw him find the thing under a tree and come running to the backdoor with it. He was holding this little blue robin's egg out to me in both of his hands. He was crying. He said it had fallen out of its nest. He wanted to save it. I tried to help him. We found some fake plastic grass and an old Easter basket in the basement and made a nest out of it. Jonathon put the robin's egg in the Easter basket and put it in his bedroom under his desk lamp to keep the little blue egg warm. I don't know how to tell him it won't be able to survive without its mother.

Dear Tommy,

Why was I the only one who could see you and talk to you? You don't have to tell me, but I'm glad that my dad couldn't see you. That meant that he couldn't yell at you or hit you too. Anyway, thank you for playing with me. I just wish that you hadn't run away from home without telling me. I wanted to go with you.

Dear Mom and Dad,

Did you know that I ran away from home when I was seven years old? I'm not sure that you knew that I was gone since I came back home in time for dinner. I would have stayed away longer, but I was afraid of what might happen to me if you had to look for me.

Watergate (1972-1974)

Watergate was a scandal that led to the impeachment of **President Richard Nixon** (for reasons that included obstruction of justice and abuse of power) and then to his resignation on August 9, 1974. It was an embarrassing episode in **American history** and many believe that the scandal led to a general suspicion of government leaders and other authority figures. *School children and other impressionable citizens didn't know who or what to believe anymore.*

[Just the first paragraph of this encyclopedia entry was torn out of Volume W of *The American Standard Encyclopedia*. It must have been Jonathon who tore part of the page out and highlighted the last sentence of the paragraph, in italics above. He was always saving pieces of paper that he seemed to think had *meaning*. (RB)]

From the Diary of Alice Bender
August 23, 1974
Robert will start kindergarten this fall. Jonathon will start the second grade. I'm glad they can both go to school so I can go back to work. Tom doesn't want me to go back to work. He won't tell me why. I think he's just worried the house won't be as clean or I won't have dinner ready for him on the days when he is at home. But I have to do something else besides staying at home and taking care of the house and the kids and Tom. I hope I find a job soon.

Dear Mom,

Thank you for buying me the cereal that had the letters of the alphabet all mixed up in it. I didn't mean to let it get so soggy that I wouldn't eat it. I kept stirring the letters in the milk with my spoon because I was trying to read the words. I thought that the letters were supposed to spell what I was going to be when I grew up.

From a Talk between Robert and Thomas

Tom: I came home from work and there was a big hole in the lawn in the backyard. I asked your brother what he was doing and he said that he was trying to dig to China. I told him that China was on the other side of the world and he asked me how deep he would have to dig. I don't know how old he was – 6 or 7 or 8. The shovel was still bigger than he was. It took your brother a while to fill that hole back in.

Dear Mom and Dad,

Do you remember when I ran into your bedroom while you were having sex? Do you remember how I was yelling, "No, no, stop, stop"? Here's what happened: I had been asleep in my bedroom upstairs and the noise had woken me up. At first, I thought that I was having another nightmare. Then, I thought that you were fighting and that you were hurting each other and that I could get you to stop. I didn't realize that that was how you made me.

From the Diary of Alice Bender
October 15, 1974
It is my first week at my new job. The mornings are a rush.
Now I realize how much I like getting the kids ready in
the morning. I like getting them their breakfast and then
getting them dressed. I like unfolding their little clothes and
laying the outfits out on their beds. They are good-looking
kids. I don't mind being a mother if I don't always have to
be a mother. I'm only working half-days. I can pick Robert
up from kindergarten when his half-day of school is over.
I like working again. I like answering the telephones and
typing up letters and filing away papers. It makes me feel as
if I am doing something.

Dear Robert,

Do you remember that snowstorm in December of 1974?
Do you remember the snowman we built like the kids did in
that TV cartoon? Do you remember how the sun melted the
snowman the next day and made his charcoal buttons fall off
his coat and his carrot nose fall off his face and his stick arms
fall out of his shoulders? I wanted him to come to life like the
one on the TV did.

[I don't remember ever making a snowman with my brother
or watching it melt. I don't think that we ever did that. But
I do remember that I didn't like to watch television with my
brother. We always fought about what to watch. (RB)]

1975

Dear Mom,

Do you remember those snow boots that I never wanted to wear to school? I made such a fuss about them because they were so heavy. They made it difficult for me to run away from the other boys who were always chasing me home.

From the Diary of Alice Bender

February 19, 1975

Sometimes I think we could be a regular, happy family. T comes home and we all sit around the dining table for dinner. We ask each other how our day was or how school was. We ask each other what we learned or what we did. We ask each other to pass the salt and the pepper or the bread. The kids help me to clear the table and do the dishes. Then we all go into the living room. We pick out a television show together. Everybody is happy while we are watching it. The kids smile and laugh for an hour or two. Then they go to bed when I tell them it's time to go to bed. T and I tuck them in for the night. Then we sit back down together on the couch until we decide to take ourselves to bed. But Tom is hardly ever at home. This has never happened in our house.

Dear Scott Poor,

I'm not sorry that I hit you over the head with my Scooby-Doo lunch box and cracked your head open with it. You were a lot bigger than I was then and I was afraid of you and I wanted you and your brother to stop picking on me on the way home from school. But here's what I want to know: did the doctor show you what it looked like inside your head? If he did, I bet it looked mean.

From a Talk between Robert and Thomas

Tom: Your brother had been fighting and he had sent some kid to the emergency room, which you probably remember. The school suspended him for that, which meant that I couldn't tell your brother that I was proud of him.

Rob: We were walking home from school together when that happened. I was too afraid to help him.

Tom: Don't tell me that.

Rob: Was that the only time that you were proud of him?

Tom: Anyway, your mother asked me to have a talk with your brother about fighting, so I told your brother that he should defend himself, but not with his lunch box. I tried to teach your brother how to fight the right way – how to protect himself with his arms and how to throw a punch by putting his body behind it – just like I did with you. Your brother covered up okay, but he was afraid to come out of his defensive posture. I kept hitting him so that he would hit me back, but it was difficult to get your brother to throw a punch.

61

From the Diary of Alice Bender
April 12, 1975
We took Robert to the emergency room today. Jonathon
was teaching him how to ride his bike. I stopped watching
them for a minute. Then I heard Robert crying and saw him
lying on the driveway with the bike on top of him. I yelled
at J to get my car keys. I picked R up and laid him down
in the backseat of the car. I backed the car up and noticed
that J was still standing in the driveway. I didn't wait for
him though. Robert was screaming. I had to get him to
the hospital. He's still there. The doctors had to put him in
traction. I don't know when he will come home. I didn't get
home until late tonight. It was after dark. J was sitting on
the front porch waiting for me. I had forgotten about him in
all of the confusion.

From the Diary of Alice Bender
April 13, 1975
This morning, Jonathon wanted to know where Robert was.
I asked him if he remembered what happened yesterday. J
said he did. But J asked me if R was really at the hospital or
if he was somewhere else. I asked J what he meant. J asked
me if R was dead. I told him R was alive, that he just had a
broken arm. J didn't seem to believe me. After breakfast, I
took Jonathon to the hospital – to prove to him Robert was
alive.

Dear Dad,

I know that I embarrassed you when you came to watch me play Little League baseball. I didn't mean to strike out each time that I came up to bat. I know that it was my fault that you didn't come to any more of my games.

From the Diary of Alice Bender
August 11, 1975
I used to make the kids stop whatever they were doing and come say hello to their father when he came home from a business trip. But eventually I figured out Tom didn't yell at them if they weren't around when he came inside the house. Now, when his car pulls up in the driveway, I send them to their bedrooms or the basement or out in the backyard if the weather is nice enough. I have explained to them how I'm not punishing them for anything when I do this. I know that I'm teaching them to be afraid of their father. I think they should be.

Dear Mom and Dad,

I wore that crown from Burger King for most of the summer of 1975 because I really thought that I was the Burger King. It couldn't have been anybody else. Nobody else was wearing a crown.

From the Diary of Alice Bender
September 2, 1975
J starts the third grade today and R starts first grade. They
will both be in school for the whole day. I can start working
full-time. I asked my boss for more hours. He says they
don't have the budget to make me full-time. I'm looking
for a new job. I know that being full-time means that the
kids will have to walk home from school by themselves. It
isn't that far. They will only be at home by themselves for a
couple of hours in the afternoon.

1976

From the Diary of Alice Bender
January 3, 1976

Tom has been at home for the last two weeks. It is getting difficult to live with him. He wants breakfast in bed. It's not room service. He won't make the bed after he finally gets up. He leaves his towels on the bathroom floor after he takes a shower. He leaves his empty drinking glasses on the furniture all over the house. This morning, he left a pair of his dress shoes outside our bedroom door. I asked him why he left them there. I wasn't going to polish them. I don't know if he remembers that I am his wife.

Dear Dad,

Do you remember when I inflated the brown paper bag like a balloon and popped it next to your head while you were sleeping? I thought that you were angry with me because I scared you. I didn't realize that what I did meant that somebody was going to die because their breath was going to go out of them.

P.S. You scared me too.

From a Talk between Robert and Thomas

Tom: I'm glad that your mother and I only gave your brother my name for his middle name. He wasn't ever going to be anything like me.

Dear Puppy Dog,

I wanted to feed you when you came to our house, but my dad wouldn't let me. He told me that you probably had rabies and that if you bit me and it broke the skin then I would have to go to the hospital to get lots of shots in my stomach. I always wanted a dog.

From the Diary of Alice Bender
March 14, 1976
I keep reading the want ads and mailing out resumes and
filling out job applications. I go on job interviews in the
afternoons. I still haven't found a new job. This wouldn't
bother me so much if Tom hadn't just gotten a promotion.
He keeps getting more of everything. I am getting more of
nothing. Tom will be responsible for more territory and more
accounts, which means more money, but it also means he
will be home even less than he already is. The money is nice.
T doesn't call home that much anymore. He says it is usually
late when he gets back to the hotel room. He doesn't want
to wake us up. I don't really believe him. I don't get as lonely
anymore. The kids are getting older. I suppose I'm used to T
being away. I have been doing it for years now. Sometimes
I even look forward to T leaving for the week. He can't do
anything to us while he is away.

Dear Dad,

I know that you were watering the lawn so that the grass
would grow. And I know that me running through the
sprinklers got the lawn all muddy and sloppy, but I wasn't
doing it because it was fun or because I wanted to make you
angry. I was doing it because I was so skinny and short. I
thought that the water falling on me might help me to grow
too.

Dear Mom and Dad,

Do you remember when I would only wear red, white, and blue clothes and shoes the whole spring and summer when I was nine years old and America was turning two hundred years old. We had learned in school about how difficult it was for America to win its freedom from England. We learned about how hard people fought and how they made all kinds of sacrifices and how lots of people died because it was so important. I liked having something to believe in.

From the Diary of Alice Bender
July 2, 1976
The kids are out of school for the summer. I'm working full-time now. The kids are at home on their own during the day. I wake them up and lay their clothes out on their beds. I leave them their breakfast on the table in the kitchen. I leave them money for their lunch on the kitchen counter. I call them during the day to see if everything is okay. Jonathon always answers the telephone. I think he waits for me to call. I worry about what they are doing while I'm not there, though. I hope they are eating both breakfast and lunch. I hope they go outside and play in the yard and get some sun. I hope Jonathon isn't just sitting inside the house and waiting for me to come home.

From a Talk between Robert and Coach Hawkins

Coach: It was Little League, so you had to let every kid play. I shouldn't have let Jonathon pitch, but I put him out there on the mound anyway. The poor kid couldn't throw the baseball very hard and that other team just pounded him. They were beating us so badly that they used the mercy rule to call the game.

From a Talk between Robert and Thomas

Tom: I put the fire out with the garden hose, but your mother had already called the fire department. The bushes and the side of the house were still smoking when the fire trucks showed up, so they hooked up to the fire hydrant and sprayed everything down some more. One of the firemen found a book of matches near the bushes and I recognized them from a hotel that I had stayed at on one of my business trips. They knew that it was arson. Your mother and I knew that it was your brother, but that was as far as the investigation went. You can still see the fire marks on the side of the house.

Dear Dad,

Do you remember that time our house almost burned down?
It was me who did it. I took the newspaper that you hadn't
read yet and I stole the matches from the pocket of one of your
jackets and I started a fire with them in the bushes that were
next to the house. I thought that it was going to be more than
a regular burning fire, though, and I still don't understand
why God didn't appear in the flames of the burning bushes to
talk to me. That isn't how it happens in the Bible and I had
some questions that I wanted to ask.

From the Diary of Alice Bender
August 28, 1976
J has been getting into trouble since I have been working
full-time. I don't want to quit my new job though. They like
me there and I need to spend time away from the house.
T and I are pretty sure J started the fire. We think he must
have done it for attention. It was on a weekend while we
were both at home. J either wanted to kill us or he wanted
us to catch him.

Dear Mom and Dad,

I know that I shouldn't have crossed my fingers behind my
back when I told you that I wouldn't steal matches or light
fires anymore. I didn't want to lie to you and I knew that I
couldn't stop doing it.

70

Dear Mr. and Mrs. Bender:

Jonathon has stopped doing his class assignments or if he does them then he gets every answer wrong, which makes me pretty sure that he does it on purpose. I kept him in the classroom today when the other kids went to lunch, but I couldn't get him to tell me what was going on with him. He seemed to think he was in trouble, even though I told him he wasn't. I'm trying to help him, but he won't let me. I don't want him to repeat the fourth grade.

Sincerely,

Miss Workman,

4th-grade teacher

P.S. Please let me know if you would like to schedule a parent-teacher conference.

[Jonathon often got into trouble on purpose. He would break things around the house – glasses, dishes, small furniture – or not come inside for dinner when he was called. He wouldn't do what he was told at school either. He would leave his homework blank even though he knew the answers and sometimes he wouldn't come in from the playground when recess was over. It was the easiest way for him to get attention. (RB)]

1977

Dear Aunt Linda,

I liked getting the mail that you sent me even if it was a chain letter, but I didn't send it off to the nine other people like the letter said. I couldn't see how the chain letter would know that it was me who broke it or how that would bring us bad luck. I could not have known that Uncle Kenny was going to get drunk and drive into a telephone pole and die in a car accident because of it.

Dear Secret Admirer,

Thank you for giving me the Valentine on Valentine's Day that asked me if I would be your Valentine. I would have been. I wanted to be. But I couldn't ever figure out who you were.

From the Diary of Alice Bender
March 23, 1977
Jonathon's nightmares have gotten worse. He often wakes up screaming. I go into his bedroom to sit with him. It reminds me of when he was a baby. I sit next to him and hold him until Jonathon realizes that nothing bad is going to happen to him. I ask him about his nightmares. He tells me about the people who turn into monsters, but it doesn't make a lot of sense. He never tells me who the people are or what the monsters do.

Dear Ted Whipple,

I wish that you hadn't moved away when we were ten years old. I know that you had to go live with your mom, but I wish that she hadn't married a guy who lived in another city.

No, what I really wish is that my mom would have divorced my dad too. Then my mom could have found me a replacement dad too. I liked playing basketball with you when you lived near me. I think that we could have won the league championship if you hadn't moved away to another school district.

From a Talk between Robert and Thomas

Tom: I was making more money and we could have moved into a nicer house in a nicer neighborhood. Or we could have bought a big farmhouse on a bunch of acres somewhere out in the country. Do you remember when we used to go for drives on the weekends and look at houses that were for sale? I wanted to move, but your mother didn't want to start your brother over at a new school. She thought that all of that change would be too difficult for him.

Rob: I don't think it would have mattered. It was going to be difficult for Jonathon if we stayed or if we moved. The other kids at school never liked him.

Tom: Anyway, we decided to stay in the same house, but I should have changed everything then. I should have bought a new house and gotten a new wife and made two new kids, maybe girls this time.

Dear Robert,

I know that Mom was always telling us to share, but I really didn't mean to give you the chickenpox too.

[This last letter is a lie. Jonathon would touch those red bumps and then pin me down and touch me with his germs. He also touched the handle on my bedroom door and he rubbed his face on my pillow. (RB)]

75

Dear Al Johnson,

I felt pretty alone standing there in that huge, open room holding my plastic tray of cafeteria food. I couldn't figure out which way to go or who to sit down with. The cafeteria was filled with so many long tables that were filled with so many other kids that I felt as if I were the only one who didn't have somewhere to sit down. I was afraid that even if there were an empty seat then the other kids at the table wouldn't let me sit in it. So thank you for letting me eat lunch with you and Bill Kendrick and Jim Washburn. I needed some friends.

Elvis Sightings (1977–)

On August 17, 1977, **Elvis Presley** was found dead in **Graceland**. There are many stories about his death, but the consensus is that he was sitting on the toilet, in the nude, and reading a magazine when he died. It wasn't long after his death that the first **Elvis sighting** took place – later in the afternoon on that same day. It is said to have happened in the foyer of Elvis's Graceland mansion. Many people still believe that Elvis is still alive and Elvis sightings continue to this day.

[Among Jonathon's other papers, I found this torn-out page from Volume E of *The American Standard Encyclopedia*. This short entry was circled, but it is unclear whether Jonathon thought that he had seen Elvis or whether he expected others to see him after his death. (RB)]

From the Diary of Alice Bender

October 16, 1977

Tom doesn't want to have sex with me anymore. I have tried dressing up sexy and also walking around the bedroom naked. He doesn't notice me either way. I have started looking through the laundry he brings home. I haven't found any stains, marks, smells, or any other kind of evidence of a woman who isn't me. I haven't found any lipstick or long hairs on any of his shirts. His clothes just smell like his cologne rather than some other woman's perfume. I have also been going through the pockets of his jackets and his pants. I have looked through his wallet and in his briefcase when he is in the shower. But I haven't found any names or phone numbers written on little slips of paper or books of matches. I did find a restaurant receipt that had two entrées listed on it. Tom claims he was just hungry and ate both of them himself. I don't believe him. He has been gaining weight though. His clothes are fitting a little tight.

Dear Dad,

I wish that you hadn't gone away on so many business trips when I was growing up. Sometimes I think that if you had seen me more often during the week then you would have liked me more than you did on the weekends when you were home. Sometimes I think that maybe you just never had enough time to get used to me.

From a Talk between Robert and Thomas

Tom: I boxed your brother's ears because he wasn't listening
to me. He was off somewhere in Jonathon-land with
his Jonathon-thoughts. I was trying to bring him
back into the real world where the rest of us people
live.

From the Diary of Alice Bender

December 11, 1977

T keeps mentioning a woman named Jane Brunson. I finally
confronted him about it. He said he works with her. I don't
believe they just work together. He says her name in too
nice a way for them not to be doing anything else together.
So I started saying things to T I wish I hadn't said. I was
yelling at him and pushing him away. He grabbed me hard
by the tops of my arms. It was scary how angry he was with
me. I don't know if he was angry because I was right or
because I was wrong or because of something else. I kept
yelling at him and he started choking me. I only stopped
yelling because I couldn't breathe. I thought T was going to
choke me to death so he could marry Jane Brunson.

From the Diary of Alice Bender
December 12, 1977
We must have woken the kids up with our fighting last
night. Though I probably didn't make much noise after T
started choking me. This morning at breakfast, I could tell
J was looking at the bruises and marks on my neck. But I
put my finger to my lips. J understands it is our secret. I put
a turtleneck on when I got dressed for work. At least there
weren't any marks anywhere on my face. And I'm glad that
it's cold outside. My clothes make sense.

Dear Mom,

There was this one time when I thought that I was having a
nightmare, but then I realized that I was awake and that it was
you and Dad fighting. I wish that I would have gotten up out
of my bed and tried to stop it. I wish that I would have been
strong enough to pull Dad's hands off your throat. I'm glad he
didn't kill you. That would have been worse.

1978

Dear Bill Kendrick,

I'm sorry that your dad died of cancer over the winter break when we were in the fifth grade. I know that you liked your dad and that you got to do fun things with him like go to ice-hockey games and go ice-fishing down at the lake. I thought about offering my dad to you, but I don't think that you would have wanted him either.

Dear Mr. and Mrs. Bender,

Your son, Jonathon, often seems distracted in my classroom. He faces the front of the classroom and his eyes are open, but he doesn't seem to be looking at anything. His classmates laugh at him when this happens and I have to say his name a few times before he blinks his eyes and remembers he is in class.

I kept him after school today. I talked about his behavior, but he wouldn't say much. That's why I have scheduled an appointment for Jonathon with the school counselor. I wanted you to know.

Sincerely,

Mrs. Farmington,

5th-grade teacher

P.S. Please sign this note and have Jonathon return it to me.

[This didn't happen only at school. It also happened at home. It could happen if we were out to eat at Burger King or Mr. Taco. It could happen if we were playing a game or watching television. Jonathon could drift away. He could disappear even if he was sitting right next to you. (RB)]

From the Diary of Alice Bender
February 4, 1978
I asked for a raise today at work. I have been a secretary there for almost two years now. My boss said he couldn't do much for me, by which he meant I wouldn't get a raise and I shouldn't ask again. I wanted to stand up and walk out of his office with my head up, except my lip started to shake and I started to cry. My boss gave me a tissue. He let me sit in his office until I stopped crying. He still didn't give me any more money. I think Tom might be leaving me. I can't take care of Jonathon and Robert on my take-home pay alone.

Dear Mrs. Farmington,

I know that I wasn't paying any attention in your class sometimes, but I want you to know that I wasn't daydreaming. What was happening was more like a blackout. I wasn't thinking or seeing anything. And I didn't remember anything after you called my name out and I came back out of the blackout. I want you to know that sometimes my mind would separate from the rest of me and take me away from people who yelled at me. Sometimes it was the only way that I could get out of a room.

Dear Dad,

They taught us in our sex ed. class that a baby lives inside its mother for nine months. So I counted the nine months back from my birthday, added on the two weeks that I was late, and figured out that I must have been conceived around your birthday, which means that one of your birthday presents turned out to be me.

Happy birthday, Dad.

From a Talk between Robert and Thomas

Tom: I had a girlfriend named Maria in Chicago and one named Clarissa in Milwaukee. Laura was in Columbus and Janice, no, Janet, was in Cincinnati. There was a woman named Tanya in Detroit, but that was only once. And once, there was this woman who was somebody else's wife and who wouldn't tell me her name. I don't know – there were more, but I don't remember all their names, or what order they came in. Your mother was always the only one in Lansing. I kept everything else out of town.

From the Diary of Alice Bender
June 5, 1978
I don't know why I'm not attracted to Tom anymore. It
could be because he isn't home much, because he doesn't
talk to me as much, because he doesn't seem attracted to
me anymore either, because he has gained so much weight
that he had to buy new clothes, because I don't like the new
clothes he bought, or because whoever he is cheating on me
with probably does like the new clothes he bought.

From the Diary of Alice Bender
July 15, 1978
I don't know what Jonathon had done, probably nothing.
Tom was angry with him though. T was yelling and J was
running through the house to get away from him. J ran out
the back door and kept running. I didn't see where he went.
He hasn't come back yet. Now it's dark. Maybe he actually
ran away.

From a Talk between Robert and Thomas
Tom: Your mother called the police, but they wouldn't
        help us to look for your brother after she told them
        that he had been having problems at home and at
        school. The police officer said that he was probably
        just at a friend's house and that he would call home
        soon. Your mother told him that your brother didn't
        have any friends, but the police officer told us not to
        worry, that your brother would come home soon. He
        said that they almost always do.

85

From a Talk between Robert and Mr. and Mrs. Hall

Mrs. H: We came home from a weekend up at our lake cottage and when we opened the garage door we saw somebody run out the side door of the garage. We could only see his legs running away as the garage door was going up, but it looked like a young boy.

Mr. H: He ran through the backyard and jumped over the back fence, but we didn't try to chase him. We think it was your brother, but we're not sure. We didn't see his face and he was running awfully fast.

Dear Mr. and Mrs. Hall,

I'm sorry for breaking into your garage with the key that you kept hidden in the flowerpot next to the side door to your garage. I know that you never liked any of us neighborhood kids on your property, but I only stayed in your garage for a couple of days. I rolled up the sleeping bag that I used and put it away where you kept it. I also threw away the candy wrappers and the bottles of pop in the trash cans that you kept at the back of the garage. I didn't meant to drink too much of your pop, but I didn't have much else to do and I was trying to keep quiet. I peed and pooped in the bucket, but I emptied it out at night and covered it up with the dirt from the garden.

I'm sorry that I didn't stop to say thank you before I ran out of your garage when you came back home. I had been waiting the weekend out until my dad had to leave on his next business trip. I was hoping that if I waited long enough to go back home then he might forget what he was going to do to me.

From the Diary of Alice Bender
July 17, 1978
Jonathon came home this morning after Tom drove away.
I was so glad he came home that I just hugged him and
made him breakfast. He was hungry and ate fast. He looked
terrible. I told him to take a shower and get cleaned up,
which he did. Then he went to bed. I tucked him in and
went to work. I told R to call me if J needed anything. J was
still sleeping when I got home. I woke him up so we could
eat dinner together. J didn't want to talk about it. I didn't
make him. I did ask him to tell me the next time he planned
to run away. I want to know where he goes. I may want to
go with him.

Dear Jimmy Ickiss,

   I'm sorry that we used to throw rocks at you and yell names
at you when you walked down the street. I know that both
the rocks and the words probably hurt you. And this apology
and explanation probably doesn't make it any better, but
we did it because you wore dirty clothes and you talked to
yourself and you lived in that old oil drum in the field behind
the school. We did it because you were different from us and
you scared us. But I want you to know that I really am sorry
about all of that. Now I understand why people live in places
where other people won't bother them.

Jonestown Massacre

912 people died on November 18, 1978 in what became known as the **Jonestown Massacre**. The story that is usually told concerns a mass suicide: 911 people drank grape **Kool-Aid** that was laced with cyanide, sedatives, and tranquilizers, and then their leader, **James Jones**, shot himself in the head.

An alternate story is that many of these people were murdered. There is a coroner's report that suggests that hundreds of the bodies had needle marks in them. This evidence fuels the theory that Jonestown was not actually a cult, but was, in fact, a mind-control experiment by the **CIA**. There are alternative explanations for everything.

See also Kennedy Assassination; UFOs; Vietnam; Watergate

[This page was torn out of Volume J of *The American Standard Encyclopedia*, but I don't think that our father was any kind of James Jones-like figure. Maybe Jonathon thought our father was running a mind-control experiment on him. (RB)]

1979

Dear Paula McDowell,

Do you remember how I used to run away from you when you would tell me that I was your boyfriend? It wasn't that I didn't like you or that I didn't like girls. It was just that I was only in the sixth grade and you were already in the seventh grade and so much bigger than me then. You already had breasts and I didn't really have anything yet. I didn't think that I would ever be big enough to be your husband.

From the Diary of Alice Bender

March 6, 1979

Tom has gained a lot of weight. It's difficult to sleep in the bed with him now. He takes up too much space. I have to fall asleep before he does and starts snoring. Whenever he rolls over, he either pulls the covers off me or pushes me out to the edge of the bed. His snoring has gotten so loud that it wakes me up. I have to wake him up to get him to stop. I have tried getting up and sleeping on the couch. T gets angry with me if I am not in the bed with him when he wakes up. Sometimes I just lie there wondering how I will be able to lie next to T every night for the rest of my life.

Dear Aunt Maggie,

I always liked you and I should have visited you while you were in the hospital, but I was afraid of catching the cancer that you were dying from. My mom told me that you had lost weight and that you had lost your hair and that you looked like a different person than the one who was her sister and my aunt. I was afraid that if I got too close to you then some of that might happen to me too. I didn't understand that your cancer wasn't contagious.

From the Diary of Alice Bender
April 26, 1979
My boss let me take all my vacation days so I could spend some of Maggie's last days with her. Earlier today, I sat in a chair next to her bed. We talked when she was awake. She was good in the morning – alert and happy. We talked about a cat we had when we were little girls. This afternoon, she didn't really move or talk much. I held her hand to let her know I was there with her. Maggie died tonight. I can't let her know anything anymore. I still have some vacation days left over. I will help Mom and Dad arrange her funeral. Then I will figure out what to do with the things she left behind. After that, I will figure out what to do with myself.

Dear Mom and Dad,

Do you remember how I always took survival supplies down to the basement whenever there was a thunderstorm watch or tornado warning? I didn't understand why everybody kept watching the television. At school, we always got under our desks and put our heads between our knees and our hands over the backs of our heads. Even the weatherman on the television would say that we should take shelter in a basement or in a ditch or in some other low-lying area. I always thought that the weatherman was trying to protect me.

From a Talk between Robert and Thomas

Tom: Your brother used to be afraid of any kind of bad weather, especially if a thunderstorm warning or a tornado watch popped up on the television screen. He would read the list of counties as it scrolled across the bottom of the television screen. If Eaton County came up, he would fill up a thermos with water and get some canned food and he would go down to the basement. I would usually tell him to come back up when the weatherman said it was safe, but sometimes I would fall asleep in front of the television. I would sleep the night on the couch and your brother would stay the night in the basement.

Dear Mr. Taft,

I didn't want to take a shower after gym class with the other boys because I was afraid to take my clothes off in front of them. I know that you had to mark me down for that, but you didn't have to let them drag me into the shower room and hold me down on the wet tiles. I was glad that the school year was almost over after that happened.

From the Diary of Alice Bender
July 26, 1979
T wasn't even home for the weekend yet when J told me he
was going to run away again. He asked me if I wanted to go
with him. I did, but I told him I had to stay home to take
care of R. J suggested R could come with us. He knew his
brother wouldn't go with us though. I helped him fill up his
backpack with food and other supplies. He told me he was
just going down the block to the Hall's garage. He said that
he wouldn't come back until T left on Monday morning. J
avoids T so much when he is home that T didn't even notice
he was gone. I had to tell him. Later that night, after T fell
asleep on the couch, I snuck out to the Hall's garage. I was
still worried about J even though I knew where he was.

Dear Dad,
   It was you who I was running away from, but I still wanted
you to come look for me.

From a Talk between Robert and Mr. and Mrs. Hall

Mr. H: We knew somebody had been living in the garage again while we had been up at our lake cottage. We didn't know then that it was Jonathon, but we didn't mind. We assumed it was somebody who needed a place to live and we already had both our house and the lake cottage.

Mrs. H:Once we learned that it was your brother, we started to make a place for him in the garage. We left a folding cot and a sleeping bag and a pillow out for him. We left a kerosene lantern and some comic books for him to read. We left an extra key for him under the flowerpot so that he could get inside the garage whenever he needed.

From the Diary of Alice Bender

September 7, 1979

T came home from a week away in Milwaukee. I said *Hello* to him when he came in the door. He didn't look at me or even respond. He carried his bags into the bedroom and unpacked and laid down on our bed and still didn't say anything. He came out of the bedroom and sat down at the table for dinner. He still isn't talking to me. If he wanted something – more ice tea or more roast beef or more mashed potatoes – then he would ask R to ask me for it. He wouldn't say anything to me directly. At first, it upset me. I couldn't think of anything I had done wrong. But now I like how cold and distant he is. I like how quiet it makes the house.

From a Talk between Robert and Thomas

Tom: She knew why I wasn't talking to her. I wasn't going to tell her. She should have apologized to me for it. She kept on as if nothing had happened.

1980

From the Diary of Alice Bender
February 4, 1980
T couldn't button up the jacket to his favorite suit this morning. He got angry with me when he saw me watching him try to hold his stomach in. I tried to avoid him. I walked out of the bedroom. He followed me down the hallway and into the kitchen. He was yelling something about my cooking. He pushed his stomach out at me and slapped it. T said I had done that to him. It was the first time he had said anything to me in a long time. All I wanted, though, was for him to stop talking.

Dear Mom,

I hope you know that it wasn't your cooking that made Dad so fat. I know that it wasn't because I used to find candy bars in the pockets of his jackets. They were usually Mars bars or sometimes Snickers, and sometimes the chocolate would be a little melted, but I used to steal them from him. Now I realize how that must have kept him from being sweet to us.

Dear Mr. and Mrs. Driscoll,

I wish that you wouldn't have caught me standing in the bushes next to your house and looking in your dining room window while you and your family were eating dinner. I didn't think that you could see me since it was dark outside, but I guess that I got too close to the plate glass window. I had never seen a family eat dinner together like that except on television. I couldn't quite hear what you were saying to each other, but it was nice to see the way that you passed the serving dishes around the table to each other.

From the Diary of Alice Bender
May 14, 1980
T has these cold sores around his lips. I know I didn't give them to him. I don't know if I will ever kiss him again. I suppose it doesn't matter. He seems to find plenty of people to kiss besides me.

Dear Mr. Sun,

Do you remember how you used to burn my skin during those summers while I was trying to grow up. People didn't know that they were supposed to use sunblock back then, but I really needed something besides the clouds that would have protected me from you.

From a Talk between Robert and Thomas

Tom: The next time that I got promoted, I moved out of the sales force and into management. It was an office job, here in the home office in Lansing.

Rob: I remember. I was glad. I thought that I was going to get to see you more.

Tom: At first, I tried to be the father and the husband that I thought I was supposed to be. After few months, I began to stay late at the office so that I didn't have to go home for dinner. I began to get up early in the mornings so that I didn't have to see you and your brother before you went off to school.

Rob: I remember, but I thought that you had gone back into sales.

From the Diary of Alice Bender
November 12, 1980
Jonathon thinks he killed his grandfather. I don't know why. I told him his grandfather had been sick with a bad heart. J keeps talking about batteries and some clock and something to do with his Walkman. I can't understand him. I think there might really be something wrong with the way J thinks.

From a Talk between Robert and Thomas

Tom: I didn't cry when I found out that my father had
died and I didn't want to go to his funeral. I didn't
feel bad for the old man or even for myself. But I
took you and your mother and your brother to the
funeral because I wanted all of you to understand
that I had become the patriarch of the family.

Dear Grandpa Bender,

I didn't want to go to your funeral after I killed you. I felt
too guilty about it, but my dad made me go and he made me
stand in front of your casket and look at you while you were
dead. You didn't look real anymore, but your face still looked
mean and I was even more afraid of you then than when you
were alive.

I had always been afraid to talk to you before I killed you,
but now I feel as if I can ask you anything. So here are my
questions for you:

(1) If you are in heaven, do you see my Aunt Maggie or
Roberto Clemente or Bill Kendrick's dad there?

(2) If you are in hell, are they saving a place for my dad?
Also, did you like my dad when he was a boy?

(3) Did you pass your bad heart on to my dad and did he pass
it on to me too? Is that why I feel this way?

1981

Dear Dad,

Thank you for leaving all the magazines with all the naked women in them underneath your bed where they were easy for me to find. I liked to look at them when nobody else was at home. That was how I first learned about women. But I have always wondered something: did you ever look at them yourself or did you just buy them for me? Were you worried that I didn't like girls?

From the Diary of Alice Bender
January 22, 1981

Now Tom doesn't come home from the office until late most nights. Tonight, he called me to tell me he has to work late, which seems considerate. I don't believe him though. So I drove through the parking lot of his office after I fed the kids their dinner. His car wasn't there. I knew it wouldn't be. I'm sure that he will smell like some strange mixture of smoke and perfume and liquor when he comes home later tonight. I know I will just lie there listening to him undress in the dark. I will try not to move too much when he slides under the covers next to me.

From the Diary of Alice Bender
May 22, 1981

T still isn't at home that much. He keeps his clothes here. He gets dressed and undressed here. He usually sleeps here too. He eats most of his meals somewhere else though – at the office, I guess. I don't know. It still feels as if he is traveling. It feels as if he has been living somewhere else for years.

From a Talk between Robert and Thomas

Tom: I liked it when I got the management job. I liked having people under me. I liked having people who reported to me, people who did what I told them to do, people who wanted to please me. That made going to work so much better than going home to you and your mother and your brother.

Dear Robin Johnson,

I don't know if you ever noticed me, but I noticed you. Actually, you were the first girl who I saw as a girl. I mean, I liked you because you were a girl and you were my age. That was why I rode my bike past your house nearly every day for that one whole summer before we went into high school. I kept hoping that you would be out in your front yard or even standing at one of the windows. I wanted you to see me on my bike with the wind blowing through my hair. I wanted you to think that I looked good that way. I thought that that might make you notice me and like me too.

Dear Anybody,

I hated my teeth when I was a teenager. My mouth wasn't big enough, so my teeth pushed against each other and overlapped in some places and left gaps in other places. I wanted braces so badly that I would lie awake in bed at night and press my thumbs against my front teeth. I kept hoping that they would look different in the morning when I smiled at myself in the mirror.

Dear Dad,

I still have a lot of questions for you. Why did you always walk around the house in the morning with just your underwear on? Why were you always scratching yourself and making that horrible noise that made all of us turn away from you? And why did you always leave the bathroom door open when you sat on the toilet? Was it because you had been living by yourself in hotel rooms and had stopped closing the bathroom door? Or were you trying to show me something about yourself?

Also, why did you tuck your shirt into your underwear when you got dressed to go to work? And why did you put so much cologne on that we could smell it even after you left the house to go to work? Was it so that we would smell it and think about you even when you weren't there? I tucked my shirt in like that once and it made me feel as if I were dressed up as somebody else and that's when I realized that I wasn't ever going to take after you.

I still wanted to be as big as you, though. I was growing as fast as a teenager could, but you kept getting bigger and fatter too. For a while, I hoped that that would make you more of a dad to me, but you just took up more and more space and got even meaner. Now I think that you were eating so much so that you would always be bigger than me.

Do you remember when I called you fat? I'm not sorry that I did that. You really were really fat. I didn't realize that you were actually listening to me, though, or that I could hurt your feelings.

I'm not trying to be mean to you. I still remember those few times that we played catch together. I used to think that throwing the baseball back and forth somehow connected us.

But now I realize that neither one of us held on to the baseball for very long. It was mostly just something that was in the air between us.

You did try to kill me a few times, though, didn't you? Isn't that why you took me to the gun safety class, so that I would know how to use your guns and *accidentally* kill myself? Or what about that time you threatened to shoot me in the middle of the night? I wasn't a burglar. I hadn't broken into the house. I was your son. I wasn't trying to steal anything from you. That was just my teenage growth spurt. My legs ached so much that they kept me awake at night. I was walking around the house to stretch my legs out and stop them from hurting me so much.

Wait, you knew that it was me, didn't you?

Did anybody ever tell you that your initials, TB, are short for a disease?

You make me sick.

Sometimes, when I fart, the smell of it reminds me of you.

That reminds me: I sometimes wished that you were dead too. I always hoped that you would die before I did.

Do you remember how you used to sit on the couch in the living room and smoke cigars in the evening? I remember how the smoke would hang up near the ceiling in the living room, but I would stay in the living room with you because sometimes you would doze off with one of those cigars still lit in your hand. I liked to watch the ashes fall on you and start all those little fires. I liked to watch the little puffs of smoke flare up as the ashes burned holes in your shirts and your pants. I kept hoping that some more of you would catch on fire.

From the Diary of Alice Bender
August 30, 1981
J's supposed to start high school next week. He doesn't seem old enough yet or ready to go. I'm worried about what all those older kids will be like. I'm worried that he will get picked on because of the odd things he thinks and says and does. High school kids can be so mean to each other. I won't be able to protect him from any of it.

Dear Mr. Ryan,

I'm sorry that I didn't submit an insect collection for your biology class and that you had to flunk me for the assignment. But I wasn't going to catch insects and then put them inside jars to suffocate them with alcohol fumes. That just made me think about how my dad smelled when he came into the house after he had been out drinking and how all of us would scatter when he tried to swat at us.

From a Talk between Robert and Thomas
Tom: I didn't hit your brother that hard. He didn't have to fall down. He was just trying to make it look worse than it was. He was always trying to make me look worse than I am.

Dear Mr. and Mrs. O'Brien,

It was me who smashed your mailbox with a baseball bat on Halloween night. I did it because my dad had hit me for not mowing the lawn even though the grass had stopped growing for the year and I shouldn't have had to mow the lawn until spring. I would have hit him back if he hadn't been drunk or if he wasn't so much bigger than me or if I hadn't been so afraid of him.

I hope that you still got your mail.

Dear Blue Oldsmobile,

I don't know if you saw me or not. I don't know if you meant to hit me or not. But it really hurt when you did it. I wish that you could have thrown yourself in reverse and turned time back for a few minutes. Maybe then you would have thought about what you were doing and you never would have hit me. Then I never would have been knocked to the ground and broken my arm and broken my bike too. Did I at least dent your fender or scratch the paint on you? I hope so.

Dear Steven Wilson,

Do you remember how you would come up behind me and knock my books out of my hand and then knock me down when I bent down to pick them up? I do. I still do. I was still afraid of you even after we graduated from high school and I went away to college to learn about the weather and you went away to jail for armed robbery. When I think about it, it reminds me of some of the stuff that my dad used to do to me. I never knew when any of it was going to happen.

Dear Dr. Fritch,

I cried when you told me that I had a cavity because I didn't want you to drill a hole inside one of my teeth and then fill it back in with some kind of metal. I hated the idea that I was already beginning to rot.

From the Diary of Alice Bender
December 5, 1981
Going to school has become difficult for Jonathon. This morning, he wouldn't even get out of bed. I called him down to breakfast a few times before I finally went upstairs to his bedroom and found him just lying in his bed. He wasn't sleeping, but he wouldn't get up. I sat down on the edge of his bed. I felt his forehead with the back of my hand. He didn't seem to have a fever, but I told him that he felt warm. I told him that he could stay home from school if he wanted. I told him I would call the school. He looked relieved. I knew he wasn't sick. He knew I knew he wasn't sick. We have an understanding. I kissed him on the forehead. That made him look as if he were already feeling better.

[I knew that our mother did things for Jonathon that she didn't do for me. It was one of the reasons that I didn't like him. She never let me stay home from school when there wasn't anything wrong with me. This was all part of Jonathon's way to get attention, but it only worked for a little while before I became the favorite again. (RB)]

1982

From the Diary of Alice Bender

January 2, 1982

Jonathon's been depressed ever since we took the Christmas tree and Christmas lights down a few days ago. I think it's because he doesn't want Christmas to be over. I made some more Christmas cookies to cheer him up – the ones with colored frosting and sugar sprinkles. When I took a plate of them up to his room, he said he wasn't hungry. I left the plate next to his bed. I don't know how to get him up out of his funk. He just stays in his bed and sleeps through meals. He sleeps through the day. He can't be that tired.

Dear Mom,

Thank you for letting me pretend that I was sick so that I didn't have to go to school. I know that you knew that I didn't really have a sore throat or a chest cold or body aches. I know that my cough sounded fake. But there really was something wrong with me. I didn't feel right and I didn't want to feel anything anymore. The only thing that felt good was sleep.

From a Talk between Robert and Thomas

Tom: Jonathon wasn't sick. He was just lazy. That's why I pulled the covers off him and pulled him out of his bed. But then he just lay there on the floor. That's why I picked him up under the arms and dragged him into the shower. I didn't even try to get his clothes off him before I turned the cold water on him. It woke him up, at least for a little while. Somebody had to do something.

Dear Mrs. Thorp,

I know that I should not have run out of your classroom when you said that there was a pop quiz. I had missed all of those classes after Christmas vacation and I hadn't read any of those chapters on the Civil War even though you sent the assignments home to me when I was sick. I knew that the war was important, but I already knew who had won.

From the Desk of Meredith Henderson,
School Counselor, Lansing School District
Wednesday, February 24, 1982

I found Jonathon sitting in a chair outside my office. He hadn't knocked on the door and nobody had told me that he was waiting there. He said that Mrs. Thorp had sent him to see me.

Jonathon stood up and I put my arm around his shoulder to walk him into my office, but he stiffened up. Jonathon asked me if he were in trouble. Jonathon said that sometimes his father would put his arm around him so that he couldn't get away while his father yelled at him. I told him that he wasn't in trouble with me.

I asked him why Mrs. Thorp sent him to see me. He said that he didn't know why. I asked Jonathon the standard questions. He told me that he only answered them because I reminded him of his mother. During the interview, Jonathon exhibited signs of depression, anxiety, and paranoia. I am recommending that Jonathon's family seek professional help for him.

[Jonathon requested his confidential file from the Waverly School District in the months leading up to his suicide. It contained this record of a meeting with the school psychologist. It seems odd that there is no record of any follow-up meetings. The school psychologist must have thought that Jonathon was getting the appropriate help elsewhere. (RB)]

From the Diary of Alice Bender
February 24, 1982
I received a call at work today from a counselor at J's high
school. Apparently, J's history teacher had sent him to the
counselor's office because Jonathon had gone running out
of her classroom yesterday. His history teacher is worried
about him. The counselor is worried about him. I am too.
The counselor gave me the name and number of a
psychiatrist. I couldn't call to make the appointment. I
don't want to do it. I think I'm going to take him to see our
regular doctor first. I don't want to get blamed for Jonathon.

Dear Waverly High School,
    I know that I should have attended you more than I did, but
I also want you to know that it wasn't you. It was the other
people who you had inside you. I saw what they did to your
windows and doors and hallways and classrooms. I saw how
mean they were to you too.

From the Diary of Alice Bender
March 16, 1982
I didn't tell T about the school counselor calling me or that
I took J to see Dr. Newman. I don't want T to have any
confirmation that there is something wrong with Jonathon.

Dear Dr. Newman,

I know that you had been my doctor for my whole life, but I was afraid to take my clothes off so that you could examine me because you were really old and I didn't want you to see me naked or for you to touch me. I did not trust you and I felt as if you were trying to take something away from me when you poked me with those thick fingers that looked like my dad's fingers. I didn't realize then that you were probably looking for bruises and scars on my body. I thought that maybe you were trying to take some of my life away from me because I was young and that was how you kept yourself alive. Then I thought that maybe you were trying to take my thoughts away from me when you looked inside my head through my eyes and my ears and my nose and my mouth.

Even after I put all my clothes back on, all those questions that you asked me made me feel as if there really were something wrong with me. Did you know what it was, and if you did, then why didn't you tell my mom and me? Or maybe you didn't know what it was or how to fix it. Is that why you told my mom to take me to another kind of doctor?

From the Desk of Dr. Allison Adler, M.D.
April 2, 1982

Patient Identification and Referral Reason:
Patient J was referred to me for a psychological evaluation by
a school counselor who was worried about physical abuse in
the home, though a family doctor reports no visible bruises
or scars. The school counselor also mentioned difficulties in
classes and problems with classmates. His mother reports that
Patient J has been sleeping more than usual and that she often
lets him stay home from school because she doesn't know
what else to do with him.

Family History and Juvenile Delinquency:
The mother reports that Patient J was an unwanted pregnancy,
a difficult baby, and that he has had difficulties in school. She
reports a history of pyromania and a history of fights. He does
not get along with his father and he has run away from home on
at least two different occasions. As an afterthought, Patient J's
mother offered that he doesn't eat well and that he never has.

Physical and Behavioral Description:
Patient J is a very thin teenage boy, though he doesn't appear
to be malnourished. His face might be pleasant if it weren't
dotted with acne and maybe if he had braces to straighten his
teeth. Throughout the session, Patient J made only occasional
eye contact before quickly looking away. He seemed anxious
and fidgety. He kept bouncing his knees up and down. He kept
picking at and adjusting his clothes, which were ill-fitting
and a little mismatched. The mother reports that Patient J is

114

often anxious or nervous around his father and that she never knows what her husband is going to say or do.

Initial Interview:

I asked Patient J why he thought he was here. Patient J believes that it is because of trouble at school or maybe because his family doctor sent him. He is not sure. Patient J reports that he has been feeling sad and that he has had "a lump in his stomach for months." He says that the feeling began "after school started" and that "sometimes it feels as if an invisible man is squeezing his chest so hard that he can't breathe."

We talked about school and his classmates, who don't like him, according to Patient J. I asked if he liked himself. He laughed oddly and said, "Not really." I waited for him to say more. Eventually, he did: "I hate the way that I feel and I hate the way that I look. I want to change everything about myself until I am somebody else."

Patient J reports that he isn't good in school and that he doesn't like to answer questions. He says that he "can't think" when a teacher asks him a question or when he has to solve a problem at the blackboard. Patient J reports that he feels like a failure in school and that he doesn't know how to do things "the right way" at home. Patient J says that it makes him feel worthless, but that he "would like to do better."

I asked him what kinds of things he is good at and he said, "Sleeping." I asked him what else. He thought for a while before saying he likes running. He said that when he runs he feels as if he "can get away from everybody," including himself. He also reports that sometimes he doesn't want anybody to know where he is.

115

His claim of being good at sleeping notwithstanding, Patient J reports that sometimes he can't sleep because he "can't stop thinking" and that other times he can't get out of bed because he is "too tired to go to school." Patient J also reports that sometimes he dies in his dreams, but that he doesn't want to die in real life.

I asked Patient J if anybody ever tries to hurt him and he told me about a bully at school named "Steve Wilson." I asked him if his mother or father were like Steve Wilson, but Patient J asked if I were going to tell his father what he had been saying. I told him that everything he said would stay with me, but Patient J shut down. I asked more questions, but our session was essentially over after that.

Diagnostic Impressions:
Patient J exhibits clinically significant distress and impairment in daily functioning – both at home and at school. The tentative diagnosis is major depressive disorder, but I will have him take the Beck Depression Inventory for confirmation.

Initial Plan for Treatment:
Therapy: 2x week for 5 weeks, then 1x week for 10 weeks.
Medication: 25 mg Tofranil, 3x a day.

Other Recommendations:
I spoke with Patient J's mother about getting him braces and maybe acne treatments – both of which should improve his self-esteem. I also spoke to her about increasing interactions with Patient J's father, but the mother was skeptical about whether that would help.

For the future, I would like to see Patient J begin interacting more with the other students at his school – both boys and girls – and for him to get involved in some kind of extracurricular activity, maybe track and field.

[Jonathon requested this confidential psychological evaluation from Dr. Adler's office in the months leading up to his suicide. What I can't believe, though, is that I never noticed Jonathon's visits to the therapist or his pill bottles. I did think it was strange that Jonathon got braces and that I didn't. That was the first time that my parents had given him something that they didn't give me too. I don't remember Jonathon's acne getting better, though. He still looked skinny and ugly to me. (RB)]

Dear Dr. Adler,

That test that you asked me to take knew how I felt. I did feel blue. I did feel sad. I did feel bored most of the time. But here is what I need to know: when I feel happy, what color will that be? Because I know that the red pills were supposed to make me feel better. But I stopped taking them because they were red and they made the whole world blurry. Sometimes, I would start to shake even when I wasn't afraid of anything. Other times, I couldn't think or I didn't know where I was. And one time, those red pills gave me red spots on my skin that made me feel prickly and hot. I thought that I had set myself on fire.

From the Diary of Alice Bender
June 30, 1982
J got his braces today. He has been smiling ever since we left the dentist's office. The braces are expensive. T didn't want to pay for them, but the orthodontist had a payment plan. I pay a little bit every month to make J smile a little more every day. His mouth sparkles, which lights up his face. That makes me happier too. I almost can't believe it. J seems like a different person tonight than he did this morning.

Dear Mom,

Thank you for paying for me to get braces even though my bad teeth were Dad's fault. Do you remember how my teeth hurt so much for that whole summer after I got my braces that I couldn't really chew food and you made me all of those milkshakes for dinner?

I remember how my face got tired because I smiled so much more than I ever had before. But that is also how I realized that when I smiled at girls, sometimes they would smile back at me. I didn't realize that the world could be such a happy place.

The other thing that helped was when you took me to the mall to buy me new clothes and new shoes. Thank you for buying me the Calvin Klein blue jeans, the Ocean Pacific shorts, the shiny Adidas sweat suit with the three stripes down the arms and the legs, the leather Nike hi-tops, and all of the other new clothes. I remember standing in front of the mirror in the dressing room and how I felt like a new person when I tried those new clothes on. I couldn't wait to wear those new clothes to school. I wanted the other kids to see the new me too.

P.S. Thank you for letting me wear my new leather Nike hi-tops out of the store. I think that I grew a few inches on that day just because those new clothes and shoes made me stand up straight when I wore them.

119

Dear Waverly High School Class of 1985,

I don't know how many of you recognized me at the start of the school year in 1982. I had new clothes and a new haircut and I felt like a new person. That's why I asked everybody to call me JT instead of Jonathon. I wanted to be the new kid. I wanted to start over and fit in and have everybody like me.

Dear Steven Wilson,

Thank you for not hitting me and picking on me in the hallways anymore. I always felt badly for Danny Wakowski, but I was glad that it wasn't me anymore. Also, thank you for inviting me to play basketball in the gym during lunch. I liked feeling included, especially by you, and I liked myself better after other people started to like me too.

From the Diary of Alice Bender
December 8, 1982
The clothes, the braces – they really seem to be working.
I think that J might have a girlfriend. At the back of one
of his notebooks, there is a page with the name "Candy"
written over and over until the whole page is filled. I hope it
isn't just that he was thinking about eating candy. T will be
relieved that J likes girls.

December 10, 1982
The Girls Who I Smiled at in the Hallways between Classes
Who Also Smiled Back at Me:

Tammy Spencer	Lisa Baer
Candace Graham	Kay Huebler
Diane Brunson	Angela Pirelli
Blinky Rush	Ginny Twichell
Marie Purdy	Rose Stringer
Claire Sherman	Rosa Vostella
Molly Simmons	Dana Tucker
Jennie Fuentes	Maxine Haller
Megan Fitzgerald	Lesley Samaras
Sharon May	Maud Siegel
Lisa Green	Barbara Mertz
Lisa Asher	Piper Reichman

[I don't believe that Blinky, Piper, Rosa, or any of the Lisas would have smiled at Jonathon, not even after he transformed himself with his new look. The girls who did like him, I think it was because they felt sorry for him. They wanted to fix him or take care of him. (RB)]

1983

From a Talk between Robert and Thomas

Tom: I tried to talk to your brother about girls. I told him to hold hands first. I asked him if he knew how to kiss. I told him the difference between putting your arm around a girl's shoulder and your arm around her waist. I told him that touching a girl's back makes her feel warm. Your brother didn't want to talk about any of it, but I wanted him to know what to do. It was one of the few times that I felt as if we were father and son.

From *End Times: A Magazine for Survivalists*
March/April, 1983

El Niño as a Sign of the Apocalypse

Mark Nichols

Nearly everybody has been talking about the weather in recent months, but most people don't recognize El Niño and its associated weather as a sign of the end times. This is, in part, because the weather experts provide certain explanations for these changing weather patterns, but colliding fronts and barometric pressure can only explain natural events such as tornadoes, hurricanes, and cyclones. Nobody has explained why beaches are disappearing along the coasts of South America or why it didn't snow in Japan last winter. And why are there more rodents and insects swarming the countryside and infiltrating our neighborhoods? These are the meek that are named in the famous Biblical saying, are they not? And what about the dramatic rise in domestic violence? As anybody with a police scanner can tell you, the people within families have set against one another in a struggle they do not understand.

This apocalyptic weather, this violence and pestilence – we are witnessing many of the important signs and we must begin to prepare ourselves for

[Jonathon only saved one page of this article – the first paragraph and then the beginning of the second paragraph. I have not found this magazine in any library. (RB)]

From the Diary of Alice Bender
March 23, 1983
Something was wrong with Tom's breakfast this morning. I still don't know what. He threw the plate at me. There was bacon and toast on the kitchen floor. The scrambled eggs stuck to the wall. It has been a while since I thought about leaving T. I need to find somewhere to live where he can't find me or the kids. And I'm not sure I can trust R not to tell his father where we go. I don't know how people leave somebody who they are afraid of. If he throws his plate at me when I make him breakfast, then what will he do to me if he finds me after I leave him?

From a Talk between Robert and Candace Graham:

Candy: Your brother changed over that one summer. He was taller and cuter when he came back to school in the fall. He smiled at me whenever he saw me and that really made me like him.

Rob: Do you remember how he asked you to the dance?

Candy: We had a class together. We sat next to each other. He wrote the question on a piece of notebook paper and handed it to me when the teacher wasn't looking. I wrote "yes" on it and handed it back to him. For the rest of the week, we walked to classes together and held hands in the hallways. I remember how excited I was for those few days before the dance.

Rob: It was a school dance, right?

Candy: Yeah, neither one of us was old enough to drive. Your mother drove us and mine picked us up. Jonathon wore a necktie and gave me flowers. We didn't dance much, though. Jonathon kept apologizing for the way he danced, especially to the fast songs, but I didn't care. I just liked being at a dance with a boy. We mostly sat in the folding chairs along the back wall and held hands. It was sweet.

Rob: What about after the dance?

Candy: My mom dropped Jonathon off in front of your house and I watched him go inside. He waved from inside the picture window and my mom drove me home. I was so happy that night and I was so excited to go to school on Monday morning. Your brother never held my hand again, though, and we never walked to classes together after that. I don't know why. I think he was embarrassed from the dance or something. I still liked him, but the rest of the school year was pretty awkward.

[Candace Graham was a year ahead of me and a year behind Jonathon. She was pretty, too pretty for Jonathon. He should have been nicer to her. I would have been. She is married now and has a different last name. (RB)]

Dear Dad,

I know that you always wanted a son who was good at baseball or football or some other sport that gets shown on television, but Coach Brackett said that I would be a good distance runner because I was tall and skinny and had long legs. He also knew that I had practice at running away from some of the other boys at school.

I liked running and not just because it kept me from getting beaten up. Running made me feel as if I could get away from everybody, even myself. Sometimes, I felt as if I could run right out of my own body.

Capital Area Conference
Track and Field Championships, May 24, 1983

2-Mile Finals

1. Thomas Hernandez, Everett	9:28.21
2. Cole Brooks, East Lansing	9:32.68
3. Mark Gibbons, East Lansing	9:44.03
4. Jonathon Bender, Waverly	9:51.54
5. Paul Barnett, Holt	9:52.37
6. Michael Brody, Grand Ledge	10:01.89

[This was a newspaper clipping that Jonathon kept from the *Greater Lansing Herald*. He had surprised quite a few people by becoming such a good runner so quickly. But our father didn't consider track and field a "real" sport. Neither did I. (RB)]

From the Diary of Alice Bender

July 11, 1983

It started as an argument about a television show. It probably wouldn't have gotten so bad if Jonathon hadn't tried to fight back. But Tom pushed him so hard that J's head snapped forward and then back into the living room wall. He slumped against the wall and sort of crumpled down to the carpet. I tried to go to J. T knocked me down too. T yelled at J to get up. J wasn't moving. It looked as if he were unconscious. When J finally opened his eyes, something flickered over T's face. He looked as if he cared or was sorry. T helped J stand up, helped him up the stairs and into bed. I wanted to take Jonathon to the hospital. But how could I explain what happened? I hope that Jonathon wakes up in the morning.

From a Talk between Robert and Thomas

Tom: I tried to make things up to your brother by teaching him how to drive. First, I took him to the school parking lot. It was big and empty and all he had to do was avoid the light poles. Then, I took him out on the country roads outside of town. There weren't many cars out there so I didn't think that he could hurt anybody but us.

Dear Dad,

I wasn't trying to drive the car off the side of the road while you were trying to teach me how to drive. I was trying to steer the car between the lines, but the way that you were yelling at me made me want to drive the car off a bridge or into a building or a tree. You were driving me crazy and I wanted it to stop.

Dear Tammy Spencer,

Do you remember all of the time that we spent together during the summer of 1983 – watching television at your house, going for walks around the block, going to the movies at the mall? How many hours do you think that we spent holding hands? Do you remember how good that felt, just holding hands? That's why I never understood why you pretended as if you didn't know who I was when we went back to school. Wait, was I just your summer boyfriend?

Dear Mom and Dad,

I'm not sorry that I snuck out of the house after you went to bed and that I took the car out even though I didn't have my driver's license yet. I'm not sorry that I didn't come home until 4 a.m. I'm not even sorry that Marie Purdy's parents called our house and threatened to call the police on me if I ever came near their daughter again. There wasn't anything that anybody could have done to me that would have made what happened that night not worth it.

Dear Marie Purdy,

Thank you for putting me in your mouth. It felt even better in there than it did in your hand and it was warmer than I ever expected. It spread this warm feeling all over my whole body and I didn't know what that was. I thought that that meant that I was in love with you.

Dear Mr. and Mrs. Evers,

It was me who egged your house on Halloween night in 1983, but I didn't realize what it would do to the paint. I should have known that those stains wouldn't wash off and that even after you painted over them that you would still think about them being there.

From the Diary of Alice Bender

December 17, 1983

Tom left. Tom left me. He left the house and left me with the kids. He didn't leave a note. I don't know where he went. Most of his clothes are gone. So are his guns. I don't know if I should tell the kids or not. I have been waiting so long to leave him. I never expected him to leave me.

1984

From the Diary of Alice Bender
January 1, 1984
It has been 15 days now. Tom didn't spend any of the holidays with us. I feel relieved, as if the pressure inside the house was released when T left us. I also feel abandoned. I didn't expect that. I can't believe how much I miss him.

From the Diary of Alice Bender

January 21, 1984

R keeps asking me where his dad is and when he's coming back. I don't know what to tell him. The first week, I said he was on a business trip. T's been gone too long for him to believe that anymore. Last week, I checked the parking lot at his office for his car. It was parked there. He's still living somewhere near here, just not with us. I've thought about trying to follow him when he leaves work. I wouldn't want T to see me doing that though. I wouldn't want him to know I cared.

Dear Dad,

Thank you for leaving us when you did. It was a while before Robert and I realized that you had moved out of the house, especially since you and Mom never really told us that you did. But after I figured that out, I liked knowing that you weren't coming home.

Dear Mom,

Thank you for taking me to the DMV to get my driver's license on my birthday. That laminated card with a bad picture of me on it was one of the best birthday presents that I ever got. I had always wanted to get in a car and just drive until I didn't know where I was anymore. I had always imagined that wherever that was that nobody there would know who I was, that I would give myself a new name, and that the rest of my life would somehow be different.

From a Talk between Robert and Thomas

Tom: I was living in a furnished apartment in another part of the city. It came with all the usual furniture that people want – couch, bed, kitchen table and chairs – plus things to cook with and eat with. I paid extra for a maid who would do the dishes, change the towels, and make the bed every day after I left for work. That place came with everything except for a wife and kids.

On the Hopefully Impending Divorce
of My Mom and Dad, Married 19 Years

Pros

1. I won't be afraid to go home and I won't get hit as much.
2. Mom won't get hit as much either.
3. I won't have to see Dad in his underwear.
4. Mom will probably be happier.
5. We won't have to wait for Dad to come home before we eat dinner.
6. Dad can't do anything bad to Robert.
7. Mom might find a nicer husband who would be a better dad.
8. We can watch the television shows that we want to watch.
9. The house won't smell like fried eggs and too much cologne.

Cons

1. We might have to move, which could mean going to a new high school.
2. Dad might try to kill us with his guns.
3. Dad might get visitation rights.
4. Mom might be sad.
5. Dad might take half of the furniture.
6. Dad might get custody of Robert.
7. Dad might remarry and make me call his new wife Mom.

Conclusion: It would be better for me – JT Bender, Aged 17 – if my parents divorced.

[I found this piece of notebook paper folded up between the pages of Jonathon's high school yearbook. I need to note, though, that my father didn't do anything to me that I didn't deserve or wasn't normal punishment. Plus, he only threatened us with a gun once that I know of. Back then, I never thought that he was actually going to shoot any of us. (RB)]

Dear Michael J. Fox or Alex P. Keaton,

I didn't like your television show even though everybody at school talked about how funny it was. I didn't think it was funny and I didn't believe that it was true that anybody's family could get along like that. I know that television is made up, but it should at least be believable. I mean, we were supposed to be about the same age, so how could our lives be so different?

Dear Dr. Ross, D.D.S.,

I really liked my new smile, but the best part was how it felt to kiss a girl after you took my braces off. I loved the way that our lips and tongues felt when Joleen Curtis could put more of her mouth in my mouth or I could put more of mine in hers.

P.S. You can use this as a testimonial in your advertising if you want.

Dear Coach Brackett,

I know that I was dying out there on the track and that everybody watching could see it happening to me as I ran down the home straight. I was trying to hold everybody else off even though I could feel the lactic acid tying my legs up and even though my body wasn't doing what I wanted it to do anymore. I know that my arms and my legs must have looked crazy the way that they were flailing. It was scary to lose control of my body and collapse before I got to the finish line. But up until that point, when the other runners were passing me in the other lanes, I was hopeful. I thought that it might somehow end differently.

From the Diary of Alice Bender
June 5, 1984
Tom called earlier tonight. I hadn't heard his voice in months. I hated everything he said. I still wanted to talk to him though – until I realized he wasn't calling for me. No, he just wants to take the boys for a weekend. He never did when he lived here. I told him I would think about it. He got angry. It sounded as if he threw the telephone across the room. It sounded so loud it felt as if he hit me in the ear. Then I heard a door slam. I sat here hoping he wasn't coming over to the house. I made the kids turn off the television and all the lights. We sat there in the dark. We pretended we weren't there for the rest of the night.

From the Diary of Alice Bender
June 29, 1984
The kids are out of school for the summer. T picked them up earlier tonight to take them for the weekend. J & R waved goodbye to me as Tom drove them away. It gave me this sickening feeling. I hope he brings them back.

Dear Dad,

Thank you for buying that case of beer for me and my friends. I know that you were just doing it because you and Mom were separated. You were probably hoping that I might like you more because of it, but I didn't. I just wanted the beer.

Dear Joleen Curtis,

I liked playing tennis with you during that one summer. It was fun to say the score at the start of a game – love, love – and think that it could mean something else. It wasn't just me saying it. You said it too.

It was strange when we went back to school in the fall and I saw you in the hallway between classes. I wanted to talk to you, but I didn't feel as if you wanted to talk to me. You looked so different in your school clothes from your tennis outfits and I know I must have too. Was that what happened? Did we just not recognize each other anymore?

From the Diary of Alice Bender
October 12, 1984
Jonathon came home drunk tonight, which I wouldn't care about so much – but he was driving my car. I'm glad he has friends and girlfriends and gets invited to parties now. I'm glad he found a way to fit in with the kids at his school. I just don't want him to kill himself doing it. I know I should discipline him. I just don't know how. T always did that. I just helped J into bed and set an empty trash can next to his bed in case he throws up. I never realized that T's violence was keeping J out of trouble and our family together.

From a Talk between Robert and Thomas

Tom: I didn't think that I would miss all of you so much since I never really did when I was away on my business trips. But after a while, I didn't want to be separated anymore. I wanted to live with your mother as man and wife again. That's why I called your mother up and asked her out on a date. I told her that I wanted to start over.

From the Diary of Alice Bender

November 17, 1984

Tom picked me up at the house tonight and took me out to dinner to a nice restaurant. He asked about the kids, about my work, about me. He asked me how I was doing, how I felt, what I wanted to do. He was sweet again. I remembered why I married him. After dinner, he drove me back to the house and walked me up to the front door. We had a short kiss. I went inside and he drove back to his apartment. It has been almost twenty years since we first went out. It felt like 1965 again.

Dear Angela Pirelli,

Thank you for taking all of your clothes off and for showing me between your legs. It was the first time that I had ever seen a real one and it was even glossier than the ones in my dad's magazines. I'm sorry for not talking to you after we had sex at your house while your mom and dad were still out to dinner. I was embarrassed about losing my virginity to you and I didn't know what to say.

From the Diary of Alice Bender

December 25, 1984

T came over for Christmas dinner earlier today. He still hasn't left. He fell asleep in front of the television after we finished eating. He's snoring. I'm afraid to wake him up. I don't want to tell him he has to go back to his apartment. I don't want to tell him he doesn't live here anymore.

1985

From the Diary of Alice Bender
February 2, 1985
Tom's lease on his apartment is up. This weekend he's
moving back into the house with the kids and me. I have
told him that it isn't going to be like it was – no yelling, no
hitting, no affairs. I am serious about these things. He is
going to sleep on the pullout couch in his home office until
I get used to him again.

Dear Dad,

I didn't lose control of your car on a patch of ice like I said. I got into that accident that dented the back fender on purpose. The only thing that I'm sorry about is that I drove back home and told you what happened. I should have just driven away from the accident and away from home and never come back. I knew what you were going to do to me when you asked about your car before you asked about me. Anyway, I wasn't hurt by the accident until you picked me up and threw me up against the living room wall. I still get headaches there at the back of my head where it put a dent into the drywall.

From the Diary of Alice Bender
March 11, 1985

Tom and I are back in the same house. We are not back in the same bed. We are not back together. I am not even attracted to him anymore. I haven't been since he moved back into the house. Now he seems so unfamiliar. I am disgusted by habits of his that never bothered me before he left me – the way he leaves his dirty clothes hanging on the furniture and the way he leaves dishes with bits of leftover food on them all over the house, all these things that he has abandoned. I wish I could get him to leave me again too.

Dear Dad,

Thank you for letting me take your car out again after you got it fixed at the body shop, but I wasn't trying to get you into trouble with Mom. I didn't know that Megan O'Malley had left her panties under the passenger seat or that Mom would find them there and think that you were having another affair. I knew that Megan had taken them off, because I had helped her do it, but I didn't realize that she hadn't put them back on.

From a Talk between Robert and Thomas

Tom: Your mother and I were still husband and wife legally, but we weren't actually husband and wife anymore. We still lived in the same house and had a joint bank account and the same last name, but we didn't act like we were married anymore. I didn't want to try anymore and I don't think that your mother did either.

145

Excerpts from Jonathon Bender's
Waverly High School Yearbook,
Compiled by Robert Bender

JT,

Remember the time that we spilled acid on the lab floor
to see it if would burn through Mrs. Bernard's class, but the
linoleum just turned a funny color and we got detention? That
was cool.

Jim Washburn

JT,

To a really good friend who helped me cheat in algebra class.
Have a good summer and keep on running.

Bob Potterman

Can I have your locker next year?

Chris Rathburn

JT,

Have a great summer and try not to die in a freak car accident
where you get decapitated like Tim Thompson did.

Joe Pennington

JT,

High school was great. I hope the rest of your life is too.

Cheryl Smith

146

JT,

I hate you so much. I can't believe you broke up with me last year.

Love, Dana West

JT,

Remember when we skipped Mr. Baker's biology class and went to The Ledges and got drunk?

Al Johnson

JT,

I really like Dana West. Would it be cool if I went out with her? She's a fox.

Steve Rigowski

JT,

You are kind of strange sometimes, but you're cute too, and that makes up for it. Didn't you ever want to make out with me? I bet you do now.

Debbie Miller

I like writing in yearbooks.

Sam Caginello

JT,

I know I shouldn't break up with you in your yearbook, but we're going to different colleges in the fall, so I think we should end it now. It will be so much more painful if we wait until August to do it.

Love, Megan O'Malley

Dear Dad,

Thank you for not punishing me for sneaking out of the house all those nights that summer before I went off to college. I used to think that it was some kind of silent consent and that you knew that I was sneaking out of the house through the sliding glass door in the kitchen so that I could go over to Megan Fitzgerald's house. I used to think that you were just happy that I had a girlfriend, but now I think that you were just hoping that I was already leaving home.

[I don't know why I never thought of sneaking out of the house that way. But I did maintain my favorite status by not getting into that kind of trouble, by not doing the kinds of things that Jonathon did. We were all waiting for Jonathon to leave. (RB)]

Dear Megan Fitzgerald,

I didn't mean to be so mean to you when I broke up with you at the end of the summer. I shouldn't have told you that I only dated you because you had the same first name as Megan O'Malley and I wanted to pretend that you were her. I should have lied. That would have been nicer.

From the Diary of Alice Bender
September 7, 1985
I dropped Jonathon off in front of his dorm today. I watched
him carry his two suitcases full of clothes and his backpack
full of other stuff into the dorm and then disappear into
a crowd of other college kids. He didn't want me to come
up to his dorm room with him. I waited in the car until he
waved to me from his dorm room window. Then I drove
away. I should probably be worried about him with all those
other kids, all of them on their own for the first time. But
he's safer away from home without me than at home with
me. Robert is next. Then me.

From a Talk between Robert and Thomas
Tom: I thought that your mother and I might get along
       better after your brother moved out. I thought that
       we might go back to being like we were before he
       was born.

Dear Professor Bartoli,
   Do you remember me? I was in your calculus for engineers
class in the fall of 1985. It was the class in that big auditorium
in Bessey Hall, the one that started at eight o'clock in the
morning. I was the one who used to bring a bowl of cereal and
a carton of milk to your class and eat my breakfast at the back
of the auditorium while you lectured.

Dear Sheri Collucci,

I wish that we had become boyfriend and girlfriend after we had sex at Jimmy Kaspar's Christmas party. I always thought that that was what was supposed to happen, so I didn't know what to think when you were holding Jim Parker's hand in the cafeteria after we came back from the Christmas break. Anyway, the thing that I remember most about that night was the way that we unbuttoned and unzipped each other's clothes, the way that we tore each other's clothes off, and how that was even more exciting than unwrapping presents.

1986

Dear Mom and Dad,

I know that I disappointed you again when I changed my major from mechanical engineering to undeclared. I know that you thought that my life would turn out well if I got an engineering degree and a good job at one of the auto plants. But I really wasn't that good at math in high school. I had to cheat on almost all those tests – crib sheets, passing answers, writing on the insides of my arms and then wearing long sleeves. I never could have gotten grades that good by myself.

Dear David Vaughn,

I'm sorry that I threw up on your towel in the bathroom that we shared. I never meant to drink that much or get so drunk that I didn't know what I was doing. I didn't want to get in a fight with you either. Didn't you know that Judy Butler had just broken up with me and that my insides were already a mess? I wouldn't have punched you in the stomach if you hadn't kept yelling at me about your stupid towel. That's also why I started dating Carol McAnallan after she broke up with you. I wanted you to feel as bad as I did.

From the Diary of Alice Bender
February 11, 1986
I haven't seen J since he started the new semester. He doesn't come home for the weekend. I wouldn't either. I wanted him to know I was thinking about him, though. I sent him a care package. It had my chocolate-chip cookies, a Valentine's Day card, and some new underwear.

Possible Majors?

~~Chemical Engineering~~	~~Large Animal Science~~
~~Electrical Engineering~~	~~Small Animal Science~~
~~Civil Engineering~~	Communication
~~Applied Engineering~~	~~Education~~
~~Advertising~~	Journalism
~~Marketing~~	~~Economics~~
~~Packaging~~	Accounting
~~Anthropology~~	~~Astronomy~~
~~Psychology~~	~~Astrophysics~~
~~Sociology~~	History
~~Social Work~~	~~Forestry~~
~~Child Development~~	Geography
Earth Sciences	~~French~~

[I found this list at the back of Jonathon's notebook for his astronomy class. My parents had been paying Jonathon's tuition, but my father wanted to stop doing so when Jonathon changed his major. (RB)]

Dear Professor Lindstrom,

The reason I took your astronomy class wasn't because I thought that astronomers who wear solar-system belt buckles are cool. It was because I wanted to be able to stand outside at night with a girl and tell her about the sky. I wanted to be able to describe the dread and the wonder that puts me in awe of my existence. And I wanted her to associate that feeling of awe with me. You might try it. It worked with Lisa Wilcox.

From the Diary of Alice Bender
May 25, 1986
This afternoon, Tom went upstairs with a bunch of boxes and started packing up Jonathon's bedroom. I thought he was doing it so Jonathon couldn't move back into the house this summer. He was. Then Tom also took all of his own clothes and things and moved himself into Jonathon's bedroom upstairs. I don't know why T just doesn't leave me again. It seems as if that would be easier. Maybe he wants to stay here to make my life difficult. Whatever the reason, there isn't any room for Jonathon inside this house anymore.

From a Talk between Robert and Thomas

Tom: Your brother thought he was old enough to stay out
        all night and drink beer with his friends. He thought
        he was going to sleep all day and stay out all night
        and do nothing all summer.

Rob: I don't remember Jonathon having friends to stay
        out and drink beer with. There may have been a
        summer girlfriend.

Tom: That's why I told him that he had to pay room and
        board if he wanted to live in my house. That's why I
        got him that summer job, so he could pay for all of
        the food he ate, all of the hot water he used, and all
        of the space he took up.

Rob: Weren't you just trying to get him out of the house?

Dear Mr. Howard,

    I'm not sorry that the cash register was short for nearly all of
my shifts that summer that I worked at your store. I know that
you never suspected me of stealing any money from you since
my dad and you were friends. But my dad costs everybody
something.

From the Diary of Alice Bender
September 1, 1986
Jonathon is still home from college for the summer break.
I'm sure that he can't wait for the dorms to reopen so he
can get out of this house again. I feel bad that he has had to
sleep in the basement all summer. I couldn't get Tom to give
Jonathon his room back. I tried to make the basement nice
though. It's dusty and damp and unfinished, but I swept up.
I set up the folding cot under one of the small windows. He
gets a little natural light down there.

Dear Dad,

Do you remember when I was leaving home to go back to
college in the fall of 1986? Do you remember how I tried to hug
you, but I couldn't get my arms all of the way around you? You
didn't know that that was the last time you were probably ever
going to see me, but I kind of did. I started laughing because
my arms weren't long enough and that made me realize that I
never loved you enough either.

Dear Simone Chute,

Do you remember that time my roommate went home for the weekend and we had my dorm room to ourselves? I do. We had those two bottles of wine that we paid a homeless guy to buy for us and we drank out of plastic wine glasses that we had to snap together to use. We stayed up all night drinking the wine and talking and making love until we fell in love with each other. I wish that we would have had more wine. Then maybe we could have kept falling into each other like that.

Dear Mom and Dad,

I know that I disappointed you again when I told you that I was going to major in earth sciences, but I have always been interested in the weather and I had decided that I wanted to be a weatherman. I know that you always wanted me to be something else. I know that you didn't think that I would ever get a job, but that's why I minored in communications, so that I could work in television. I was trying to make myself marketable and I already knew that I was good at forecasting.

Dear Dad,

I'm not sorry that you cut off your own ring finger when your wedding ring got caught in the teeth of that chainsaw. I'm glad that you had to experience that kind of physical pain and I hope that you really felt how much it hurt and that you didn't pass out from the blood loss or anything like that. I didn't want you to miss any of the pain. But here's what I want to know: did you know that that was a sign? Did you know that Mom was going to divorce you after that happened?

Dear Laura Thorp,

I'm sorry that the rubber broke and that I came inside you. I didn't realize that it had happened until I saw some of me coming out of you. But I'm glad that you didn't get pregnant. I wouldn't have known how to be a father then.

I understand why you broke up with me after your period came. That blood was a relief to me too.

1987

From the Diary of Alice Bender
January 23, 1987
R got his acceptance letter earlier today. He can go to MSU
just like J. R says he doesn't want to go though. I told him
he can be undeclared or change his major ten times, but he's
going to college. I told him that he was getting a chance I
never had. I just want him to move out of the house though.
Then I can move out too. I'm not leaving anybody behind
except for Tom.

[I didn't want to go to MSU. I didn't want to keep following
Jonathon through school, but it was the only school that
accepted me and I knew that my mother wanted me to go.
I thought that she wanted me to go for me, though; I didn't
realize that she wanted me to go so that she wouldn't feel
guilty about leaving my father. At least Jonathon and I lived
in different dorms and had different classes and different
majors. I didn't have to see him. (RB)]

Dear Mary Craftman,

When I saw you talking to Greg Holiday, I thought that you were getting him ready to be your next boyfriend. He was laughing and you were laughing and then you both looked over at me. I thought that you going to break up with me right then and I couldn't let that happen. That's why I left the party without you and that's why I broke up with you by calling your room and leaving a message with your roommate.

Dear Leo Moore,

Why didn't you come back to school after spring break? The rumor was that you were having an affair with a married woman and that her husband found out about it and pushed you off a hotel balcony in Florida. I don't know where that story came from, but it wasn't in the newspapers.

I still remember when a woman who must have been your mom came to get your things from your dorm room. I wanted to ask her what had happened to you, but she looked too sad. That's why I helped her carry your things down to her car. Wait, you are dead aren't you?

March 7, 1987
Professor Lipaski
Geography 203, Introduction to Meteorology
Lecture: Families of Clouds

1. Clouds belong to different families. Said another way, certain clouds are related to each other. Other clouds are simple precursors, but not related to each other. So maybe that was the explanation. Maybe I really wasn't his son.

2. Cirrus clouds are thin and wispy (my mom), indicating that a storm may be in the distance.

3. Cumulus clouds develop vertically. Their tops are often brightly lit by the sun, but their undersides are often dark and shadowed (me).

4. Stratocumulus clouds cover the sky in non-conforming layers and folds that are scattered with dark patches. They often form in the wake of a cold front and may produce snow.

5. Nimbus clouds are low-hanging and overbearing and thick enough to blot out the sun (my dad). Rain or snow continuously falls from them.

[These class notes are excerpts from one of Jonathon's college notebooks. I don't know why he kept them. I didn't keep mine. Also, most of them are somewhat worn, as if Jonathon had continued to study his notes. Maybe he was looking for clues. As you can see, even clouds reminded him of our father and our family. I am not mentioned, though he may have intended to relate me to the stratocumulus clouds. (RB)]

Dear Amanda VanderMere,

I know that we had only known each other for a weekend when I asked you to move in with me, but that weekend was the best two days of my life up to then and we both needed somewhere to live next year. You seemed so perfect to me then and I think that I did to you too. I didn't want to live half of the next year in your apartment and half of it in mine. I wanted us to be in the same place as much as we could. I wanted to be with you so much that I didn't even want to sleep. I used to miss you for the few minutes while you were away from me in the bathroom.

Remember how we stayed up the whole first night talking and touching? Remember how we used up that three-pack of condoms and in the morning we had to go to the corner store for more of them? Remember how we both quit work that next week so that we didn't have anything else to do except to be together? We both took out more student loans and moved into that little one bedroom apartment that was off-campus.

We slept on a mattress on the floor and had sheets for curtains and we were so happy. Our furniture was furniture that other people were throwing out. We had a little kitchen table with wobbly legs that was where we ate our meals, but it also doubled as a desk. We had those two chairs that were mismatched because one of them was yours and one of them was mine. We had that love seat that we found on the sidewalk and carried four blocks back to our apartment. I loved that furniture and that summer and you. I wish that I could meet you again right now and that we could be at the beginning of something again.

Dear Brian Knott, Assistant Manager,

Thank you for mailing my last check to my house for me even though I didn't call in sick or ever come back to work at Kroger's grocery store. I needed the job and I needed the money, but I couldn't bring myself to put any more price tags on any more jars or boxes or cans of food. Pulling the trigger on the pricing gun made me think of shooting my dad and I thought that I might actually do it.

From the Diary of Alice Bender
September 8, 1987
I dropped R off at Holden Hall today and helped him move into his dorm room. I told him to take anything important with him. I didn't tell him why. I couldn't tell him I was leaving his father or how it might not be safe for him to go home for a while. I hope him being in college – the classes, the girls, the parties – will keep him from thinking about his family or going home.

I am taking all of my sick days and all of my vacation days together. T is leaving on a business trip for a week. J is coming to help me move out. I am taking my clothes, some of the furniture, the things that were mine before I married T, old family photographs, new family photographs, and anything else that might remind T of me. I want it to seem as if I never lived in this house or with him.

Dear Amanda VanderMere,

Thank you for letting my mom move in with us when she was in hiding from my dad. I know that you thought that it would just be us living together. I did too. And I know that we were never the same after my mom started sleeping on the loveseat that we had found, but she couldn't leave the apartment without being afraid and I didn't want her to be afraid anymore.

Dear Robert,

I'm glad that you moved out of the house and that Dad couldn't do anything to you anymore either. I know ▮▮▮▮▮▮▮▮▮▮▮▮▮▮▮▮▮▮▮▮▮▮▮▮▮▮▮▮▮▮▮▮▮▮▮▮ ▮▮▮▮▮▮▮▮▮▮▮▮▮▮▮▮▮▮▮▮▮▮▮▮▮▮▮▮▮▮▮▮▮▮▮▮ ▮▮▮▮▮▮▮▮▮▮▮▮▮▮▮▮▮▮▮▮▮▮▮▮▮▮▮▮▮▮▮▮▮▮▮▮ ▮▮▮▮▮▮▮▮▮▮▮▮▮▮▮▮▮▮ I know that you must have been afraid not to. I would have been too. I was too. I wish that I would have been big enough or strong enough to stop him then, but I couldn't help you or Mom or even myself then.

[I blacked this passage out. Jonathon and I disagree about our father and our childhood, but this passage is too much to let stand. My father never did anything to me like what Jonathon suggests. (RB)]

From a Talk between Robert and Thomas

Tom: I knew that something had changed when I pulled
         into the driveway and your mother's car wasn't there.
         Your mother wasn't inside the house and there were
         other things missing too. There were empty closets,
         empty hangers, empty drawers. Certain pieces of
         furniture were gone. There were a lot of things missing
         from shelves and walls – photographs, souvenirs, all
         of the mirrors. The sets of dishes, sets of silverware,
         and sets of glasses – they were all broken up.

Rob: How do you think I felt when you left us?

Tom: I didn't know what to do, so I set the table for the
         whole family – me, you, your mother, and your brother.
         I was going to make a big family dinner, but when I
         opened the refrigerator door I saw that your mother
         had unplugged it before she left. All of the food had
         gone bad – sour milk, moldy fruit, soft vegetables,
         gray meat – everything inside it was rotten.

Rob: Are you just going to ignore my question?

Tom: I didn't talk to anybody for a long time after all of
         this happened. I tried to find your mother, but I
         didn't know where to look. I went to her parents'
         house and her sister's house. I looked for her car in
         driveways and in the garages of people she knew.
         I tracked down her boyfriends from high school
         and a guy she dated before she met me. I staked out
         where she worked. I drove up and down the aisles of
         parking lots at apartment complexes looking for her
         car. I looked inside the windows of apartments to
         see if I recognized any of the furniture.

165

Rob: (*stares at Tom*)

Tom: Sometimes, I just drove up and down the streets of Lansing hoping to find her driving her car. Once I saw a car that was the same color and the same make as hers. I looked through the windshield as it drove past, but it wasn't your mother. Either that or your mother had become somebody I didn't recognize anymore.

Rob: When you were driving around, what were you going to do if you found Mom?

Tom: (*looks away from Rob*)

Rob: Did you know that Jonathon was sick again then?

Tom: (*no response*)

Rob: Did you just want to know where Mom was living?

Tom: (*still no response*)

Rob: Did you take your guns with you when you went out to look for her?

Tom: (*looks back at Robert*)

Rob: You weren't thinking about killing her were you? (*pause*) I can't believe that Jonathon may have been right about any of this.

Tom: (*looks away from Robert*)

Rob: I'm leaving.

From the Diary of Alice Bender
October 4, 1987
Jonathon and Amanda are both at class. I get scared when they aren't here with me. I'm afraid to go outside. I'm afraid to pull the edge of the sheet back and look out the window. I hope they come back soon. I find it reassuring to see how much two people can like each other.

Dear Grandma Bender,

I didn't come to your funeral because I knew my dad would be there too. I wanted to see you, but I didn't want to see him, and I didn't want him to see me. I couldn't risk him following me back to my apartment and finding my mom there. I didn't want her to be dead too.

December 3, 1987

Professor Martine
English 202, Introduction to American Fiction
Paper Proposal

This paper will analyze suicide as a plot device in such novels
as *The Awakening* by Kate Chopin, *Appointment in Samarra*
by John O'Hara, *The House of Mirth* by Edith Wharton, and
Lie Down in Darkness by William Styron. It will focus on
the fictional life events that led up to each fictional suicide
and discuss the methods of suicide as a thematic reflection of
character.

*Interesting topic, but please see me during my
office hours.*

[The following piece of paper was folded up in the back of
one of Jonathon's college notebooks. It is the first time (that I
know of) that Jonathon thought of suicide in such detail. The
handwritten note is, presumably, from Professor Martine.
(RB)]

From a Talk between Robert and Professor Martine

Rob: My brother was Jonathon Bender. He took a course
         of yours in the fall of 1987.

Prof. M: Jonathon Bender?

Rob: He might have called himself JT.

Prof. M: I'm sorry, but I don't remember him.

Rob: You might have talked with him during your office
         hours about his paper proposal on novels about
         suicide.

Prof. M: I saw lots of students during office hours.

Rob: Well, I'm interested in a term paper he would
         have written for your class.

Prof. M: I don't keep papers that long.

Rob: Why did you teach novels about suicide?

Prof. M: (*hangs up*)

[This telephone call took place on April 25, 2000 at 3:00
in the afternoon. Professor Martine still teaches literature
courses at Michigan State University. (RB)]

Dear Amanda VanderMere,

Your note was in a red envelope and it had my name written on it in pretty handwriting, so I thought that it was some kind of Christmas card that you had made for me. I never thought that my parents' failed marriage would cause us to fail too. Was that really the reason? I didn't realize that my dad still had so much influence over my life. I thought that I had gotten away from him. Do you remember how happy we were at the beginning of us? I never realized that you became unhappy until it was the end of us.

Dear Mom,

I missed you after you moved out and got your own apartment, especially since I couldn't talk Amanda into moving back in with me, especially after she wouldn't talk to me anymore. I thought that you moving out might convince her to come back too, but it didn't. Now I don't have anybody.

1988

Dear Anybody,

I was afraid to leave my apartment. I didn't want Amanda to come back and me not be there. The only people I talked to were the people who answered the telephone when I called to order food and the only times I opened the door were to pay for the food when it was delivered.

I stopped taking showers because I was afraid that I might not hear Amanda knock on the door when I was under the water. I wore the same clothes over and over again after it became too difficult to decide if my shirt matched my pants and, eventually, I became used to the smell of myself.

Before long, it became difficult to move, so I mostly stayed on the loveseat. Sometimes I sat up and sometimes I laid down. I noticed when it was day and when it was night by how much light came into the room around the edges of the sheets that I kept pulled closed over the windows.

Sometimes I laid my head on the armrest and that made me think of Amanda holding me.

I was so tired.

Have you ever felt that way too?

Dear Landlord at Cedar Village Apartments,

I'm so glad that you let yourself into my apartment with your master key. I knew that some time had passed, but I didn't know how much. I didn't realize that it was 1988 or that January had passed and the new semester of classes had already started. I didn't realize that I hadn't paid the rent or that I didn't even have enough money to pay the rent.

If you hadn't found me, then I might not have ever left my apartment. I was so afraid of anything outside of me. I felt as if I had cracked somewhere inside of me and even though I wrapped my arms around my legs and tried to hold on to myself, the crack kept getting taller and wider until there was an opening where you could see through me if you looked at me. Even now, I can feel that opening getting bigger inside of me and pretty soon I will disappear into it.

From the Diary of Alice Bender
February 1, 1988
Jonathon's landlord called me. I was his emergency contact
on his lease. He wouldn't tell me what was wrong over
the telephone. I wasn't prepared for what I saw when I let
myself inside Jonathon's apartment with my old key. The
floor was covered with empty pizza boxes, empty containers
of Chinese food, plastic forks, and dirty napkins. It smelled
like Jonathon was rotting. I knew that he had fallen into
a deep depression again. I called out Jonathon's name. I
found him under the covers in his bed. I helped him into
the shower and got him cleaned up. I got him dressed in
some clean clothes and drove him to the university clinic.
I wanted to take him back home with me. The doctor
wouldn't let me. They are keeping him overnight for
observation so Jonathon doesn't kill himself.

Dear Man Who Looked at Me through a Face-Sized Window
Every Half-Hour,
    I know that you were just looking in on me to make sure
that I wasn't trying to kill myself. I know that you were just
checking to see that I was still alive at 1:30, at 2:00, at 2:30, etc.,
but I liked seeing your face in that little window and I started
to wait for you to appear. I found it reassuring.

From the Desk of Dr. Thomas Morris, M.D.
February 1, 1988

Patient Identification and Referral Reason:
Patient JTB was brought into this clinic by his mother who
says that Patient JTB has not been attending classes and may
not have left his apartment for over a month. The mother and
the patient both report that he has a history of depression and
that it was successfully treated in the past by medication and
therapy.

Physical and Behavioral Description:
Patient JTB is a good-looking young man, though it does not
appear as if he has been taking care of himself. His hair is
unkempt, his skin terribly pale, and his eyes almost hollow.

Initial Interview:
Throughout the session, Patient JTB mostly mumbled his
answers to my questions. His movements were slow. From
what I could gather, his girlfriend broke up with him and that
was the trigger for the current depressive episode, though
the separation of his parents may also have some bearing.

Patient JTB also reports: "I knew what was happening to
me because it had happened to me before." He said that he
could feel himself "slowing down," and that it was difficult
to move or get out of bed. Patient JTB further reported that
he "wanted to stay under the covers so that nobody would
see me." He also said: "I don't want to be me anymore. I
don't want to be anybody else either."

Diagnostic Impressions:
Patient JTB exhibits clinically significant impairment in daily functioning. The diagnosis is major depressive disorder. There may also be some dissociative aspects to the disorder.

Initial Plan for Treatment:
Therapy: 1x week for 8 weeks.
Medication: 20 mg Fluoxetine, 1x day.

Other Recommendations:
I have provided doctor's notes for all of Patient JTB's professors and recommend that he attend his normal schedule of classes. The focus required to make up his class work should help to relieve his depression. I also recommend that Patient JTB find a new girlfriend.

[Jonathon requested this confidential psychological evaluation from Dr. Morris's office at the University Clinic in the months leading up to his suicide. I had no contact with Jonathon during this time of his life. I didn't even know that our mother had been living with him for some of that time. I cannot confirm or deny any of this, though the whole scenario seems doubtful to me. (RB)]

Dear Kelly Hagan,

I know that I shouldn't have asked you to move in with me on our first date, but I was depressed and my medication wasn't working yet and I needed somebody to replace Amanda. I really think that we could have been happy together, at least for a while.

From the Diary of Alice Bender
June 14, 1988
Jonathon's medication seems to be working. He made it through the semester and passed all of his classes. He has a summer job and a new girlfriend. I'm so proud of him. I'm proud of me too. I have a new apartment and a new boyfriend too. Of course, I don't know why I'm so hopeful. None of it has worked out for either of us before.

Dear Mr. Darnell,

I don't blame you for firing me, especially since I didn't sell any of your water softeners to any of the people who I cold-called for you. I could never say any of the script that you gave me to say. I kept thinking that the person who answered the telephone was expecting me to be somebody who they knew, somebody who they would want to talk to. I knew that when I told them who I was that I would be a disappointment to them.

Dear Heather Fairing,

I'm sorry that I wouldn't open the windows in our apartment even though we didn't have an air conditioner and it was so hot that summer that we lived together. I was afraid that somebody was going to climb up the fire escape and break in on us while we were sleeping and I didn't know what they might take. There was already too much that was missing from us.

Dear Ellen Lipsyte,

You probably thought that it was me who kept calling you and hanging up after we broke up. It was. I wanted to see whether you were at home at night or whether you were already going out with somebody else. I was glad that you kept answering the telephone.

From a Talk between Robert and Thomas

Tom: Your mother and I divided nearly everything. We each got half the house and everything inside it. We each got half the money and half my pension. I got the family photos with me in them and your mother got the ones with her in them. I gave your mother all of Jonathon and asked for all of you in return, but your mother wouldn't do it. That's how I only ended up with just a quarter of my kids from my marriage to your mother.

From the *Greater Lansing Herald*, December 25, 1988
No Official Explanation for Lockerbie Tragedy
Charles Leckel, Newswire

LOCKERBIE – It has been four days since Pan-Am Flight 103 exploded over Lockerbie, Scotland and there is still no official explanation for the tragedy. There was no distress call and officials are still looking for the black box.

As it fell from the sky, the airplane broke into smaller and smaller pieces. All 259 people on the airplane died. The passengers probably lost consciousness when the air pressure changed after the explosion. If not that, then the sudden change in air pressure would have caused their lungs to swell and then collapse.

11 more people on the ground died when the wings and the fuselage landed on a neighborhood street, causing houses to explode. One surviving resident said, "I thought we were being attacked by the Germans."

It is days after the tragedy and parts of the plane, luggage, and bodies remain scattered all over the streets and gardens of the small town of Lockerbie. One surviving resident said, "I covered up a man and a woman who landed in my back garden with blankets. I set two matching pieces of luggage next to them. I hope somebody comes to take them home."

Eventually, authorities are expected to tag all of the bodies and body parts. Officially, nobody has claimed responsibility for these deaths.

[This may be why Jonathon stopped using any form of transportation for a while. (RB)]

179

1989

Dear Mom and Dad,

I know that you had to sell the house when you got divorced. I know that you couldn't just split the rooms up or do a timeshare or anything like that. But I don't think that you should have sold it to that young couple. The same thing was probably going to happen to them.

Dear Professor Moubray,

I really liked your class on broadcast news. I liked writing the news stories and the way that we had to condense them down to 3 minutes or 30 seconds. But I especially liked being on camera and delivering the news. I liked sitting at the news desk with the pages in front of me. I liked the idea of being broadcast to so many people. It made me feel important.

Dear Florida State University,

I applied to your graduate program in meteorology because I wanted to be near the hurricanes. I also applied to Iowa State University for the tornadoes and San Jose State University for the earthquakes, but they didn't let me in them either. All I wanted was to move to somewhere where there was bad weather. I didn't know what to do after you and everybody else rejected me.

Dear Debbie Stornant,

I never told you this, but I was hoping that you would notice me looking up at the sky. I was hoping that you would ask me what I was looking at and that it would give me an opportunity to tell you all I know about clouds. I was hoping that it would make me look dreamy and reflective and I was hoping that you would like that. I'm glad that you did, at least for a while.

Mix Tape for Debbie Stornant

Side A (Slow)
1. 'Hello' by Lionel Richie
2. 'I Want to Know What Love Is' by Foreigner
3. 'Can't Fight This Feeling' by REO Speedwagon
4. 'Every Breath You Take' by The Police
5. 'Flashdance… What a Feeling' by Irene Cara
6. 'Together Forever' by Rick Astley
7. 'I Just Died in Your Arms' by Cutting Crew

Side B (Fast)
1. 'She Drives Me Crazy' by Fine Young Cannibals
2. 'I Feel for You' by Chaka Khan
3. 'Straight Up' by Paula Abdul
4. 'Dress You Up' by Madonna
5. 'Addicted to Love' by Robert Palmer
6. 'Need You Tonight' by INXS
7. 'Love Song' by Jonathon Bender

[I found an old mix tape with everything else that Jonathon left behind. I tried to play it, but the tape spooled out and self-destructed in the cassette player. The cassette had a label on it, though, and a list of songs. I don't know what the last song was or if Jonathon wrote it or sang it. I don't know whether Jonathon ever gave the mix tape to the girl or whether she gave it back to him. (RB)]

From the Diary of Alice Winters
June 10, 1989

J graduated today and that makes me so happy. I never thought that he would make it this far – that he would get past his father, his depression, himself. I watched him walk across the stage and get his diploma. I watched him throw his cap into the air with all of the other kids who graduated. Afterward, I took him and his girlfriend out to a nice restaurant for dinner. J told me that he's going to take the first weather job he gets offered. J and Debbie are going to move wherever that is. I don't want him to leave. But I hope he does.

Dear Dad,

I stopped sending you Father's Day cards on Father's Day because I didn't think that you wanted to be reminded that I was your son anymore. I have been trying to forget that there is one day every year that is designated for you and me and our relation to each other.

Jonathon "JT" Bender
5812 Park Lake Road
East Lansing, MI 48823
(517) ███████

EMPLOYMENT OBJECTIVE
To analyze and forecast the weather for a media outlet or weather service. (I also own a car and am willing to chase storms and tornadoes.)

EDUCATION
B. S., Michigan State University. June, 1989.
Major: Earth Sciences. Minor: Communications.
Diploma, Waverly High School. June, 1985.

WORK EXPERIENCE
Temporary Worker. The Temporary People Agency.
June, 1989 to present. Supervisor: Mrs. Elizabeth Vogel.
Many short-term jobs with duties that included typing, filing,
making long-distance phone calls to ex-girlfriends, looking out
the window, and stealing office supplies.

Phone Sales Associate. Softer Water for Everyone, Inc.
June to July, 1988. Supervisor: Mr. Terrence Darnell.
Duties included dialing phone numbers, talking to people I didn't
know, and listening to the dial tone.

Stock Boy and Bag Boy. Kroger's Grocery Store.
June to July, 1987. Supervisor: Mr. Brian Knott.
Duties included pricing and shelving items for potential
consumers, and carrying bagged items to consumer vehicles for
home transport.

Cashier. Howard's Hardware Store.
June to August, 1986. Supervisor: Mr. Henry Howard.
Duties included receiving company monies in exchange for
company goods and diverting funds into personal accounts.

Dear *Greater Lansing Herald* Want Ads,

Do you remember when I used to look at you every day? I used to circle some of your job listings and then make phone calls or send out resumes. I always thought that I was going to find my future by reading you, but I couldn't ever figure out what you wanted me to do.

Dear Mr. Gardner,

I'm sorry that I stopped coming to work, especially since I told you that I would stay on for at least a year if you gave me the job. I did need a job and money, but I was trying so hard to be myself back then and I couldn't figure out how selling lighting on commission was going to be some part of me. I didn't realize until later that that job could have made me feel electric. Anyway, I'm sorry that you had to find a replacement for me, but people have had to do that for my whole life.

Dear State of Michigan,

Moving away from you that fall after college was easier than trying to run away when I was little. I had a car by then and could drive.

P.S. If you talk to any of the other states, please don't tell my dad where I went.

1990

[This year is missing. I don't know what happened to it or if it ever existed for Jonathon. I know that Jonathon had moved away from Michigan, but I don't know where he went or if he had found a job that he wanted to do. He may have already been in Missouri, but I can't be certain about that. He didn't write any letters for this year, and there aren't any diary entries from my mother about Jonathon either. He wasn't talking to my father, of course, and 1990 was before he met Sara or started working for WEXJ. I just hope that he wasn't institutionalized without anybody in our family knowing about it. (RB)]

1991

Dear Jane Thompson,

Do you remember when you made breakfast for us after that first night that we spent together? I liked you, but I couldn't eat the fried eggs because the smell of them reminded me of my dad standing at the stove cooking breakfast in his underwear, which meant that you standing there in your underwear also made me think of my dad standing there in his underwear. That's why I broke up with you. It wasn't because of the way that you chewed your food like I said.

Dear Mr. Roberts,

I don't know why I couldn't sell enough life insurance for you to keep me on with your agency, but people seemed to think that I was too young to understand the bad things that can happen in a lifetime. I could never convince them that I already knew too much about bad weather and accidents and death. I could never convince them that we should all buy as much insurance as we can afford.

Dear Tornado,

I don't know if you will remember me, but I was the guy who was chasing you in his car. You kept cutting across all those empty fields and I kept driving through all those stop signs out on those country roads. I was trying to get close enough to you to shoot you with my video camera. I was trying to get footage that was good enough to show on television. I was using you to get an interview at a television station. Plus, I thought that if I kept chasing you then you would eventually die out and leave everybody alone. Anyway, thanks. I got the job.

What to Do in Case of Flooding

If you live in a floodplain, then you may want to stockpile sand and sandbags to build floodwalls. If flooding still occurs, then you should move to higher ground or to the upper floors or even to the roof of your residence. Before doing so, you should shut off all utilities and disconnect all appliances, unless there is already standing water.

You should not drink tap water after flooding occurs. It may be contaminated. Instead, think ahead and stockpile bottled water before any flooding begins. You may also wish to fill your bathtubs and sinks. Please note that your bottled water should be stored above ground, so that it cannot float away.

If you need to flee, then beware of water that moves. You can be swept away by a surprisingly small amount of flowing water, even an automobile can. Instead, you may want to use a small watercraft, such as a canoe or a rowboat, if one is available, or, if not, then build a raft.

[It appears that Jonathon started to write a book sometime in the early 1990s. There is a notebook titled *Surviving the Weather and Other Disasters*. The table of contents lists chapters on blizzards, hurricanes, floods, drought, tornadoes, earthquakes, pestilence, childhood, and the apocalypse, though it appears that Jonathon only wrote two excerpts and that he never finished the book. (RB)]

What to Do in Case of an Earthquake

An earthquake is not technically weather, but you should know how to survive one anyway. Avoid anything that can break or fall – including windows, exterior doors, exterior walls, overhead lights, and tall furniture such as bookcases or entertainment units. If you cannot take cover under something, then you should sit in a corner with your knees pulled into your chest and your head between your knees. You should cover the back of your head and neck with your arms and hands.

It is better to be outside than inside during an earthquake, though you should still stay away from anything that could fall on you – including trees, houses and other buildings, telephone poles and other things connected to wires, as well as the sky. If an earthquake has caused a visible rift in the earth and you find yourself separated from the rest of the world, then do not attempt to leap across the rift, which is almost certainly wider than you realize and may cause your disappearance.

If you are buried under the results of an earthquake, then please do not attempt to dig yourself out. You may cause even more debris to shift and press down on you. You may also create dust clouds that will make it difficult to breathe and shorten your life if you do survive. Instead, wait. Make small, repetitive noises such as tapping. Hopefully, rescuers will hear you and dig you out.

Dear Mr. McComb,

I know that you hired me at WEXJ because my resume said that I had a master's degree in meteorology from Florida State University, even though I didn't. I couldn't even get into graduate school there. But I really wanted to be the weatherman. I knew that if I could just get you to hire me then you would never fire me after you saw how I could influence the weather. Ever since I was little, I could cough or sneeze and make the wind gust or a thunderstorm begin to form. I can cry and make it rain.

So thank you for letting me be the weatherman on the weekends and when Veronica Dixon was on vacation. I also liked being the one who reported on the weather from remote locations. I can still see myself holding an umbrella in one hand and my microphone in the other hand. The camera is rolling and I feel as if I am keeping the rain off everybody who is watching me.

Dear ESPN,

Thank you for airing all of those baseball games on television. I used to come home late after a news broadcast and watch the West Coast games when nearly everybody else in my part of the world was sleeping. Watching all of those people gathered together in those stadiums always made me feel as if I were part of something grand.

From the Diary of Alice Winters
November 12, 1991
I received a package from Missouri in the mail today. I
had no idea who it was from until I recognized Jonathon's
handwriting on the envelope. My stomach dropped when
I opened it and saw that it was a videotape. There wasn't
a letter or anything else with it. My first thought was that
Jonathon had killed himself, that it was his last will and
testament. Of course, I didn't have a VCR to play the
videotape. T got that in the divorce. I had to buy a new one
and R helped me hook it up. It was an incredible relief when
I realized what was actually on the videotape – J's weather
reports from every weekend for the last few months. I was
so happy that I cried. I went from thinking he was dead to
being so happy that he was kind of famous in Missouri. It
had never occurred to me that J had actually gotten a job in
television.

Dear Veronica Dixon,

I liked being on camera and doing the weather reports
every weekend. I liked knowing that so many people were
watching me even if I didn't know who most of them were.
But sometimes, when I was just living my regular life, I felt
as if people were watching me then too. Did that ever happen
to you?

1992

Dear Weather Satellite,

I didn't know many people when I first moved to Jefferson City. That's why I used to watch you blinking your way across the sky at night. It made me think that you were winking at me and that made me think that we were friends. That's why I climbed up onto the roof of my apartment building every night to look for you – even if it was cold, even if there were clouds. I was comforted to know that you were still traveling in your orbit around me.

Dear Kathy, Paula, Robin, Tammy, Candace, Marie, Megan, Lisa, Angela, Piper, Joleen, Dana, Andrea, Megan, Sheri, Mary, Judy, Carol, Simone, Laura, Amanda, Kelly, Heather, Ellen, Debbie, Jane, and anybody who I have forgotten,

Thank you for breaking up with me, letting me break up with you, or never going out with me. If you hadn't, then I never would have met Sara.

From Sara's Eulogy for Jonathon

I recognized Jonathon from the television, which made me feel as if I already knew him, which made me smile at him as if I already knew him. He smiled back at me. We were always connected to each other after that.

Dear Sara,

You were so beautiful the first time I saw you that the first thing I thought was that I wasn't good enough for you. I still don't know why you thought I was. But thank you for smiling at me so that I could smile back at you. Out of all of the thousands or even millions of women I had ever seen or met, you were the one who I picked out of everybody else.

From Sara's Eulogy for Jonathon

Our first dinner together was at a French restaurant, and I remember how Jonathon told me he liked the way I ate my food. He said I smiled while I chewed and that made me feel beautiful. Toward the end of that meal, he reached across the table and touched my arm and I felt a warm rush go up the length of my arm and fill up the rest of my body.

Jonathon and I could look at each other and tell what each other were thinking. At first, it was just a way of being intimate. We were only thinking about each other back then. But later, Jonathon began to believe that he could tell what other people were thinking too. That was the first sign of his paranoia that I recognized.

Dear Residents of Jefferson City, Missouri
and the Surrounding Areas,

I'm sorry about sometimes interrupting your television shows to bring you a weather report, but I only did it when there was a weather watch – which meant that a tornado or flooding or some other kind of hazardous weather was possible – or if there was a weather warning – which meant that some kind of hazardous weather was actually occurring. I only did it because I cared about all of you. I was trying to save everybody.

Dear Sara,

   One of the things that I liked about you was the way that you would stop to pet the dog that somebody else had left tied up outside of a restaurant or a grocery store. You always made me feel better about being abandoned by other people too.

Seven Natural Wonders

The Grand Canyon, Arizona.
Rio de Janeiro Harbor, as approached from the ocean, Brazil.
Iguassu Falls, Argentina.
Mt. Everest, Tibet and Nepal.
The Nile River, Egypt.
The Northern Lights, the Universe.
Sara Olson, Jefferson City, Missouri.

[I found this poem written on the back of a photo that shows Jonathon and Sara smiling. It isn't clear from the photo where they are, and Sara couldn't remember where the photo was taken, but they were probably on vacation. They look so happy in the photo that I wanted to include it here, but it has been withheld at Sara's request. (RB)]

1993

Dear Sara,

Thank you for moving into my apartment and living there with me. I needed somebody else to sit on the couch and the chairs with me. I needed somebody else to watch the television with me. I needed somebody else to eat at the kitchen table with me. I needed somebody else to put their clothes in the dresser drawers and the closet with my clothes.

THE EXTENDED FORECAST
FOR SARA'S BIRTHDAY
AND THE FOLLOWING YEARS

BENDER WEATHER SERVICE
JEFFERSON CITY, MISSOURI
7:00 P.M. CDT WED APR 21 1993
AFTER A PROLONGED PERIOD OF HAZARDOUS
WEATHER AND STORMY RELATIONSHIPS UNSEA-
SONAL GULF WINDS COMBINED WITH ABOVE
NORMAL TEMPERATURES HAVE STATIONED AN
UNEXPECTED WARM FRONT OVER THE AREAS
OF JONATHON AND SARA. BE ADVISED THAT
EVEN BETTER CONDITIONS ARE EXPECTED
TO DEVELOP OVER THE COMING YEARS. THIS
WARMING ADVISORY WILL BE IN EFFECT FOR
THE FORESEEABLE FUTURE.

[I found a birthday card that Jonathon made for Sara. I don't
know why he had it and she didn't, but it had this made-up
weather report written inside it. Maybe he asked for it back
in the divorce. I'm told that he hated it when his forecasts
were wrong. (RB)]

From Sara's Eulogy for Jonathon

There are some things I want you to know about Jonathon. He had a difficult childhood, but he was a kind man. He always wanted to be a father, even though his father didn't want to be one to him. He always felt like the littlest guy in any group, but he was actually quite tall. Jonathon had nice hair and soft skin, and he was nice and gentle with me too. I liked it when he smiled. We were both happy when he smiled. I tried to get him to do it as much as I could.

Unfortunately, I didn't really start to see Jonathon's mental illness until we started living together. He had been able to hide certain behaviors from me when we were just going out on dates or just staying over at my apartment or at his place. But the more time I spent with him, the more I started to notice when he wasn't the Jonathon that I had known so far. There were days when he couldn't get out of bed and there were times when he couldn't talk, not even to tell me what was wrong. And often, he would get distracted by airplanes flying overhead, especially if they left a trail of smoke across the sky. He would watch until the airplane was gone and the smoke had dissipated and disappeared. In retrospect, I'm sure that he was often somewhere else, but those were the times that I noticed he was gone.

Dear Sara,

I always liked the way that you would unbutton your shirts and unzip your skirts when you came home from work. I always liked it whenever you changed your clothes in front of me and I saw some of you naked. And I liked that you didn't wear any underwear under your summer dresses when it was really hot during the summer.

Dear Old Woman,

I don't know if you are still alive or if you will remember me if you are, but you were sitting one table away from me in the Main Street Diner, and you seemed to close your right eye every time that I looked at you. I thought that you probably recognized me from the television and that you were winking at me, but then I realized that you couldn't help it. I realized that you had had a stroke and that you couldn't really move that side of your face. I wish that you really would have been winking at me, though, and I wish that all of me worked too.

Dear Residents of Jefferson City, Missouri
and the Surrounding Areas,

Do you remember that snowstorm that shut down our whole town for a few days in early December of 1993? I knew that it was coming, but there wasn't anything that I could do to stop it. I turned the heat up in my apartment and opened all of the windows, but I couldn't make it hot enough to turn the snow into rain.

All of the kids seemed happy that they didn't have to go to school and I remember how nearly everybody traveled by skis or by sled. Most of our cars were buried under the drifting snow and it looked as if we were living in a different time and a different place. It reminded me of when I was born.

1994

Dear Sara,

We should have visited your Grandma Olson in her nursing home in Florida while she was still alive. I know that she had Alzheimer's disease and that she probably wouldn't have known who we were, but she would have known that somebody had come to visit her. The only reason that I never suggested it was that your mom and dad always talked about her in the past tense. I thought that she was already dead.

Dear Sara,

I didn't want to take the Christmas lights down until long after Christmas was gone. I liked the way that they blinked off and on. It reminded me of how much fun we had together that weekend that we went to Las Vegas even though we lost so much when we were there. I never expected that leaving those Christmas lights up so long would cause us to lose even more of us.

Dear Sara,

I wish that you never would have said yes when I asked you to marry me. I wish that you wouldn't have let me keep asking you to marry me. You had the answer right the first few times.

From Sara's Eulogy for Jonathon

I always felt lucky to have met Jonathon and to have lived with him for the years that I did. Jonathon believed in luck too, both good luck and bad luck. He had a lucky hat. He would never open an umbrella inside the house. He would cross his fingers and knock on wood. Jonathon once told me that he always wanted a dog when he was a kid and that he was going to name it Lucky, but his parents would never let him have one.

Jonathon was also superstitious. If he dropped a knife or a fork, he would wait for me to pick it up. He said it was bad luck if he picked it up himself. He would open all of the windows and doors in his house if somebody died. Sometimes these sorts of things got confused with his mental illness.

Dear Residents of Jefferson City, Missouri
and the Surrounding Areas,

I know that it didn't rain through the late spring and early summer of 1994 and that the growing season was stunted by the drought. And, yes, I was the weatherman, but it wasn't my fault. I tried to seed the clouds to make it rain. I took long showers and left the sprinklers on outside my house. I even peed outside. I watched sad movies to make myself cry. I tried to make water any way that I could, but my influence was limited to small areas around my body and my house.

Dear Sara,

I know that I often acted overwhelmed with work, but that's only because I was. The atmosphere was exerting a pressure of up to 40,000 pounds on me and I had to work really hard to use the body pressure that I had inside me to keep myself from collapsing on myself.

Harold and Carol Olson
invite you to the wedding of
Sara Elizabeth Olson
and
Jonathon Thomas Bender
on Saturday, September 10, 1994
at seven o'clock in the evening
at Hermann & Sons Home Association Ballroom
2637 South Saint Mary's Avenue
Jefferson City, Missouri

even though we do not wish for
our daughter to marry this person
she is our daughter
and this is what she thinks she wants
so we are going along with it
and trying to act happy about it
even though it makes us sick

[I found this wedding invitation with Jonathon and Sara's marriage certificate and divorce papers. Presumably, Harold or Carol Olson wrote in the words in italics, though my mother suggests that the handwriting actually looks like Jonathon's. (RB)]

From a Talk between Robert and Thomas

Tom: Your brother didn't invite me to his wedding, but I
      wouldn't have gone anyway. I wasn't going to buy
      him a present and I didn't want to see him happy
      either. That's not how I remember him. Besides, your
      mother probably would have been there too and I
      didn't want to see her either, happy or otherwise. Do
      you remember when I wasn't talking to any of you? I
      was pretending that none of you existed back then.

From the Diary of Alice Winters

September 10, 1994

Sara looked beautiful. I cried at the ceremony. It is such
a huge relief that Jonathon found somebody who would
marry him. J seems so much more normal with Sara. I
wonder if she knows about his depression. I hope she will
be able to take care of him.

Dear Sara,

   Thank you for making me put a sliver of our wedding cake
under my pillow on our wedding night. It made a big mess,
but I had the sweetest dreams of you. I just wish that our
honeymoon in Aruba hadn't been for only that one week. I
wish that it would have been for the rest of our lives.

From Sara's Eulogy for Jonathon
Jonathon often fiddled with his wedding ring, turning it around and around his ring finger with his thumb. He said that doing it made him think of me.

Dear Sara,

Do you remember that old mattress that we slept on when we first met, the one that sagged in the middle? I always liked the way that we would roll over into the middle of the bed in the middle of the night and roll into each other. I always liked the way that we woke up in the morning, how we had to work extra hard to separate ourselves and get out of bed. We never should have bought a new bed after we got married.

1995

From Sara's Eulogy for Jonathon

We looked at a lot of old houses before we bought the one on Riverside Drive. It was just after the bend in the Missouri River straightens out and sometimes we would sit out on the back porch and listen for the boats going up and down the river. You could hear their horns, the boats calling out to each other as they passed each other going different ways.

Dear Sara,

I never told you this, but this old house that we bought, the one that I'm still living in, I liked it because of its address – 1947 Riverside Drive. That was the year that my mom was born and I had the idea that living in a house that was numbered for that year would somehow give me a new life.

It did for a while, didn't it?

From Sara's Eulogy for Jonathon

We didn't have much furniture in our old apartment, so the house felt so empty when we moved into it. In that first year in the house, we filled all of the rooms with furniture and rugs and things on the walls. That made it so that there wasn't as much echo in any of the rooms, so that Jonathon couldn't mistake that kind of noise for voices.

Dear Sara,

I never thought of this until now, but all of this furniture that we bought, it used to be trees.

Dear Sara,

Do you remember how we stained our expensive new couch by having sex on it right after it was delivered? Do you remember how we had to turn the cushion over to hide it? I turned the cushion back over after you left me and left me with the couch. It reminded me of how excited by each other that we once were.

That makes me think of how much you wanted to have children. I did too. That's why I was always disappointed when your period came every month. I have always thought of all that blood as one of my failures. I really thought that we were going to have one kid and then another kid. I thought that the kids would get bigger and that we would eventually move into a bigger house. I thought that our kids would have kids and we would become grandparents together. I thought that we would retire and then take care of each other. I never expected so much of that to never happen to us.

Did you know that we never developed the film from our vacation to the Grand Canyon? I just found the camera a few days ago and the roll of film inside it wasn't finished, but I got it developed anyway. They were almost all photos of us with the canyon behind us and we are almost always smiling. Do you remember? We were happy. Unfortunately, the photo shop also processed the unused film at the end of the roll, so the last few photos are all just black, which made me realize that they were actually photos of all the things that we never did together.

From a Talk between Robert and Mr. McComb, News Director of WEXJ

Mr. M.: One night we had fifteen seconds to fill and Jonathon was asked to stretch out the weather forecast. I'll never forget it because instead of saying that tomorrow would be a good day for having a picnic or something like that, Jonathon said something like this: "Most people don't believe it yet, but global warming is really happening. The sea levels are rising and eventually we are all going to drown." Our broadcast was live, but we work on a delay, so we had enough time to cut it. I think we played music instead.

1996

Dear Sara,

Sometimes I wonder if I should have patched that crack in the wall of the foundation. Sometimes I wonder what would have happened if our house had really flooded. Maybe we could have started our marriage over again.

I want you to know that I always tried to keep us dry. I tried to patch the leaking roof of our new old house. I can't even remember how many times I went up there – the buckets of tar, the new metal flashing and matching shingles. I don't know why nothing worked, especially since I was the weatherman and I should have had enough influence over the snow and rain to keep you dry. I really was trying to keep the bad weather off us. You knew that, right?

Dear Grandma and Grandpa Winters,

I'm sorry that I didn't come back to Michigan for your funerals. I know that you didn't know that I wasn't there, but I wish that I could have given both of you some of my years, the ones that I'm not going to use, so that you could have lived together for a little while longer. Anyway, I miss you and I will see you as soon as I'm done writing these letters to everybody.

Dear Sara,

I smashed the television screen with a hammer because I thought that it was watching us. Even when it was off, I could see this faint reflection of somebody in the screen. Also, I unplugged the radio because I thought that it was listening to me and broadcasting everything that I thought outside my head. But even after I unplugged the radio, I could still hear them talking. That's why I threw the radio outside in the rain where it probably got electrocuted.

What I'm trying to say is thank you for holding on to me so tightly when I couldn't hold on to myself anymore. Sometimes, I can still feel your arms around me trying to hold me still.

From Sara's Eulogy for Jonathon

Jonathon's depressive episodes became psychotic and paranoid. His reality became different from my reality. Sometimes he heard voices that I did not hear. Sometimes he would hold his hands over his ears, as if he were trying to shut something out, but I think he ended up trapping the voices inside his head.

There were also times when Jonathon didn't even recognize me as his wife anymore and thought that I was a stranger or somebody breaking into our house. I always thought that I should have left him during one of those psychotic episodes, that it would have been easier for Jonathon if a stranger had left him rather than his wife, that he wouldn't have missed me if he didn't know who I was.

It was so difficult to take Jonathon to the hospital to have him admitted. I had to admit that Jonathon's mind had started to fail after our marriage had started to fail. I tried to hold on to him. I tried to bring him back to himself and to me and to our marriage, but eventually I didn't know where to look for Jonathon inside Jonathon's mind.

When I left him at the hospital, he looked back at me as the orderlies took him away. He looked like a child who was being abandoned and didn't know why and I felt sick. I felt as if I had given up on him even though I had done everything for him that I could. Jonathon was everything to me and then he was too much.

Dear Sara,

Thank you for taking me to the mental hospital and checking me into it. I'm sorry that I cried and that I made you cry when you had to leave me there. It was so hard to be separated from you when I was also separated from myself.

From the Diary of Alice Winters
March 31, 1996
J's Sara called me today. She told me that she had had Jonathon admitted to the hospital. She said that the doctors weren't allowing any visitors yet though. I have to wait to see him until the medication turns J back into some semblance of himself. For years, I have been hoping that this wasn't going to happen to him again. I have been waiting for when it would.

Dear Anybody,

At first, I stayed in a white room. People dressed in white brought me pills and they watched me swallow them. They brought me food and I had to eat all of it. They looked in my mouth afterward.

The people dressed in white blended back into the color of the walls and disappeared. They kept me locked in my white room, but I don't remember doing anything wrong. Nothing else happened except when Dr. Gregory was talking me into getting better.

Eventually, they let me leave my white room, but I had to do the same thing at the same time every day – get up, get dressed, eat, take my pills, talk to Dr. Gregory, eat, take my pills, watch television in the day room, eat, take my pills, get undressed, go to sleep. The only thing that changed was sometimes Sara came to see me in the afternoons. Also, I remember my mom coming once, but I'm not sure whether she was really there. She may have only been real to me.

Dear Dr. Gregory,

Thank you for writing a new prescription for me. I think that it helped that the pills were red. That seemed to stop some of the voices from talking to me.

From the Diary of Alice Winters
April 16, 1996
I saw J today. He has turned into a tired, smaller version of himself. He moves slowly. It is difficult for him to remember things. It is like he is already an old man. He reminds me of my father before he died. The doctor explained that it was the medication doing that to Jonathon, that he expects him to return to normal as soon as they reduce the medication. J looks a long way away from normal. I knew this was going to happen. I just didn't think it would be this bad.

Dear Mr. McComb,

I know that I shouldn't have called in sick for over 100 days in a row. I know that I didn't have that many sick days and that my vacation days and my personal days ran out too. But I couldn't figure out how to get out of the hospital. The doctor that I talked to kept telling me that I couldn't really influence the weather, that nobody could, and I kept explaining to him how I did it. I even showed him, but when he didn't believe that my coughing caused a gust of wind, then I realized that he wasn't going to release me until I agreed with him, so I did.

Thank you for letting me come back to work at WEXJ. Getting back on camera made me feel alive again.

Dear Sara,

Thank you for taking me back home and taking care of me. I know that I wasn't myself anymore, but I wasn't sure that I wanted to be.

From Sara's Eulogy for Jonathon

The doctor gave me the instructions for Jonathon's medication and told me that his mental illness was worse than any side effects could be. I'm sure that that was true, but those pills made it so Jonathon couldn't sleep and we couldn't have sex. He gained weight and almost always had a stomach ache. He was often anxious and agitated. He didn't like to stand up because he was afraid of getting dizzy. I thought that Jonathon would be better than he was when he came home. He wasn't psychotic anymore, but he was sick in different ways. Still, the worst part was that I had to take Jonathon back to the hospital once a week for a therapy session with his doctor. This was always difficult. I always had to reassure Jonathon that I wasn't going to commit him again.

We tried to start over. We tried to start our marriage over, but Jonathon was never the same person after he came back home. He lost his personality and he didn't even seem to be trying to find it. No, that just sounds mean. But he looked down so much after he came back home. It made me angry that I couldn't get him to look at me.

1997

Dear Sara,

 I'm sorry that I stopped coming to bed at night and started sleeping on the couch with the television on. I liked it when the local television station went off the air and all that static came on. It blurred how badly I felt.

From the *Jefferson City Chronicle*, May 28, 1997
Cult Group Seeks New Way to Get into Heaven
Francine Kuehn, Newswire

SAN DIEGO – 39 members of a cult that called themselves Heaven's Gate were found dead in a house in Rancho Santa Fe, California. The cult members drank a lethal dose of vodka that was mixed with depressants, then placed plastic bags over their heads to hasten the end of their lives in what was an apparent mass suicide.

The suicide note explained that they expected their souls to board a spaceship that was flying behind the Hale-Bopp comet as it traveled past the Earth. They all wore identical black-and-white sneakers, though it is unclear whether they thought they would have to chase the spaceship. As of press time, it is unknown whether their souls made it on the spaceship or not. We do know they left their bodies behind.

Dear Residents of Jefferson City, Missouri
and the Surrounding Areas,

I wish that that tornado hadn't touched down and destroyed most of the houses on Market Street and Lime Kiln Road. I wish that Mr. and Mrs. Akers hadn't died and that so many other people weren't hospitalized. I wish that everybody would have stopped watching me on the television and moved to their basements or to an interior closet. I also wish that the tornado hadn't taken my thoughts and twisted them all up too.

From Sara's Eulogy for Jonathon

I couldn't get Jonathon to say anything to me after I told him that I was going to separate from him. I couldn't get him to look at me either. All his breath seemed to go out of him. He started crying and there wasn't anything that I could say to get him to stop. I started crying too and I kept asking him to please say something to me. Eventually, Jonathon said that he wanted it to stop raining outside so that we could stop crying so that we could still be together. But it kept raining.

Dear Sara,

I didn't help you move out of our house and into your new apartment because I wanted you to leave. I did it because I wanted to see where you were going to live. I wanted to be able to imagine you being happy there.

But I wish that I would have been one of the things that you had taken with you when you moved out of our house. It would have been like you were leaving me for me and we could have started over.

From Sara's Eulogy for Jonathon

I still loved Jonathon, but it was an extinct version of him, and I couldn't bring that Jonathon back to life. Now, when I think about his whole life, not just the time that I was with him, I think Jonathon probably died a few times before he finally killed himself.

To-Do List: Monday, September 1, 1997

1. ~~Call Sara and let her know that I found her blow dryer under the sink in the bathroom.~~
2. ~~Wait for Sara to come and pick up her blow dryer.~~
3. ~~Think about Sara while I'm waiting for her.~~
4. ~~Look around the house for other things that are Sara's.~~
5. ~~Wonder what Sara is doing.~~
6. ~~Remember some of the things that Sara and I did together.~~
7. ~~Miss Sara.~~
8. Miss Sara some more.

[I found this "To Do" list posted on Jonathon's refrigerator. It must have been there for years. (RB)]

Dear Sara,

Did you know that to separate also means to break, to break up, to come apart, to cut off, to detach, to disconnect, to discontinue, to divide, to divorce, to leave, to part, to rupture, to sever, to split, to split up, to uncouple, and to undo? I looked it up because I was trying to understand what was happening. I realized that it wasn't just happening to our marriage and to us. It was happening to me too.

From the Diary of Alice Winters
September 10, 1997
Sara called to tell me she left J last week. She says he isn't doing very well. I have called J. He says he can't talk and hangs up whenever I tell him it is me. After a few rounds of this, he said he didn't want to tie up the line. He thinks Sara might be trying to call him. J said he thinks it is Sara every time the telephone rings. He is disappointed every time it isn't her. I will wait a while before I call again. I don't want to make this worse.

From Sara's Eulogy for Jonathon
Even after I moved out of our house, I would still check-in on Jonathon. I would sit in my car at the end of the block just to make sure that he made it home from work at night.

Dear Sara,

I used to walk around the house looking for things that you had left behind – clothes, a blow dryer, the pillow that you liked to sleep on – so that I would have an excuse to call you up and see you. But it wasn't long before I couldn't find anything else in the house that was yours. That's when I started buying things that you used to use so that I could pretend that you had left them behind – your favorite shampoo, that one kind of hand lotion, blue jeans and shoes that were in your size.

Do you remember the last time that you came over to pick up some of your things and I followed you out to your car and then I followed your car to the end of the driveway and then I followed your car down the road? Do you remember how I kept waving goodbye to you as you drove away from me? I kept waving until I couldn't see your car anymore, but I wish that I hadn't done any of that. Now all I can see is you leaving me.

1998

Dear 917 Ionia Street,

I don't know if you recognized me since I was just a little boy when my mom and dad sold you in 1971, but I drove back to Michigan to see you. That was me all grown up sitting in the car that was idling across the street. I was looking for some of my childhood and I thought that you might know where it is.

MISSING PERSON
SARA BENDER

(aka Sara Olson)
(aka My Sweetie)

Dob: April 21, 1970.   Sex: Female.

Height: 5'8".   Weight: 135 lbs.

Hair: Pretty.   Eyes: Bright.

Last Seen: Driving away from me.

Reward: Anything you want.

Contact: Please contact me at (573) ███████████ with any information that might lead me to Sara or that might stop me missing Sara.

[Among Jonathon's other papers, I found a stack of "Missing Person" flyers that had a photograph of Sara on them. I have not included the photograph at her request. It is unclear whether Jonathon received any response to the flyer or even whether Jonathon ever posted these flyers in Jefferson City or elsewhere. (RB)]

Dear Mr. McComb,

I don't blame you for firing me for not coming into work anymore. I thought about calling in sick, but then I thought that I had probably used up all of my sick days for my whole life. But thanks for my severance package. I lived on it for the rest of my life.

From Sara's Eulogy for Jonathon

I used to get a lot of telephone calls at night, and I assumed that they were from Jonathon, but he never said anything after I said hello. I wouldn't hang up, though. I would stay on the line and we would listen to each other breathing. That was the only way that we could still be together.

Dear Sara,

I hate the fact that I don't know what you are doing right now. You might be happy. There isn't any way for me to know whether you are or not.

Dear Brown Squirrel,

I'm sorry that I ran over you with my car. I thought that you were going to stay on the other side of the road. I didn't expect you to double back on yourself.

Dear Dr. Gregory,

I know that I wasn't supposed to stop taking my medication, but I didn't think that those little pills were big enough to fix everything that was wrong with me or save me. They were so small.

Dear Sara,

I didn't answer the telephone when you called because I had stopped talking to anybody but myself. But thank you for leaving the message about our divorce papers on the answering machine. I have been playing it over and over ever since you left it – not the whole message, just the part where you say, "Hello, Jonathon. It's me, Sara." It reminds me of when we first met.

1999

Dear Sara,

I hope that you will think of me when you check to see what the weather is going to be like on any tomorrow. I hope that you will think of me when you feel the sun on your face or when you forget your umbrella and get caught out in the rain. I hope that you will think of me when the wind blows through your hair or when you are cold and wrap your arms around yourself to keep yourself warm.

From Sara's Eulogy for Jonathon

I wish that Jonathon had always taken his medication. I wish that he were still alive. I wish that he were still my husband and that I were still his wife.

Dear Sara,

I didn't sign the divorce papers because I wanted to be married to you for as long as I could. I was even hoping that you wouldn't be able to divorce me at all if I didn't sign them. You didn't have to go to a judge to prove that I was unfit for marriage.

Since we really are divorced now, I think that we should split up our memories too. I want the time when we met and the time when we went to the Grand Canyon. You can have our first date and the day we got married. You can also have the day when you left me, which I have no use for. I want when we moved in together and when we bought our house, though, and I want all of the times that we sat on the couch and watched television together. You can have the times we ate breakfast together, but I want most of the dinners. There are a lot more. Maybe we should talk about all of them.

Possible Ways to Make Myself Feel Better
January 27, 1999

1. Overdose on some kind of pills (supposedly, the whole body contracts painfully).

2. Jump off of something high — a bridge, cliff, building, etc. (I'm afraid of heights).

3. Drown myself in the Missouri River or some other body of water (I might float away and never be found).

4. Drive off of a cliff (the airbags might save me).

5. Hang myself from the rafters (it would remind me of my dad choking my mom).

6. Breathe natural gas (the oven doesn't work).

7. Breathe carbon monoxide from my car exhaust (I can listen to the radio).

The Last Will and Testament
of Jonathon Bender

I, Jonathon Thomas Bender, of Jefferson City, Missouri, do make and declare my last will and testament as follows:

To my mother, Ms. Alice Winters, should she still be living after my death, I leave enough money so that she may buy a necklace or a scarf, so that she might have the feeling of something nice around her neck. I also leave to her my remaining tranquilizers, pain pills, and mood enhancers should she find them useful. I further leave to her, and thankfully so, the happy moments of my childhood, of which she was so much a part.

To my father, Mr. Thomas Bender, should he still be living after my death, I leave my physical pain – including any bruises, welts, cuts, or broken bones – as well as all of the emotional pain that started with him and hopefully ended with me. I also leave him any of the thoughts and the behavior that I inherited from him, including any violent tendencies, any destructive tendencies, and any lack of kindness. I further leave to my father the sound of my breathing, any smell associated with my bodily functions, and any fluids or substances that came out of my body after I died. I even further leave to my father my refrigerator, though its door should be removed so that no children are hurt by it. Finally, I leave to my father enough money so that the grass over his grave may be tended meticulously for eternity.

To my brother, Robert Bender, I leave the loss of my memory so that he may begin to forget the things that our father did to us. I also leave to him my box of crayons and anything else that was left over from our childhood. Finally, I leave to my brother Robert my car, so that he may drive as far away as geographically possible from where we grew up while still remaining in a warm and sunny climate, which is probably somewhere in Central America.

To Scott Poor, should he still be living, I leave the Scooby-Doo lunch box that I cracked his head open with and which should now be a collector's item.

To my dead Aunt Maggie, I leave my pancreas and my liver and any other internal organs that she might have found useful, so long as they are not cancerous, except for my brain, which I leave to Steven Wilson, because he was a stupid bully.

To Ted Whipple, should he still be living, or to his son, should he have one, I leave my good leather outside basketball, and the hope that he plays the game the way we used to play it – all day long and even after dark until our mothers called us home.

To any childhood neighbors whosoever may still be alive – including but not restricted to Mrs. McCoy, Mr. and Mrs. O'Brien, Mr. and Mrs. Evers, and Mr. and Mrs. Hall – I leave a lump sum, to be determined by and dispersed as my executor sees fit, to cover the cost of the repairs of or the replacement of anything of theirs I might have damaged or vandalized – including but not restricted to doors, windows, mailboxes, garages, and paint jobs.

To Sheri Collucci, Marie Purdy, Angela Pirelli, Megan O'Malley, Laura Thorp, Amanda VanderMere, Debbie Stornant, and any other ex-girlfriends, named or unnamed, I leave the explanation contained in the letters to them. Additionally, to Heather Fairing, I leave a portable air conditioner and a portable heater so that she may feel comfortable all year round wherever she is living.

To WEXJ, I leave the weather van that we drove to chase storms, along with all of its radar equipment, even though none of it was mine. The keys are inside the glove box.

To the weather in general, I leave my house and my household goods, which includes all items not specifically designated elsewhere in this last will and testament, the only provision being that the windows and the doors of the house should always remain open and that no attempts to paint, repair, or care for the house in any way should ever be made.

For my self, I leave this instruction: that my body should be cremated. My hope is that once my body takes the form of ashes I will be warm forever. To help facilitate this wish, I ask that my ashes be placed in an urn made of a heat-conducting material that shall remain under a heat lamp.

To Kathy Granger, I leave $2 per hour, to be paid by my executor, so that she can babysit my ashes and check on the warmth of the lighting as often as she is willing or finds necessary.

To Sara Olson, my ex-wife, I leave any other money remaining in my bank accounts after the above wishes are fulfilled, and do so with the hope that it can purchase some kind of happiness for her. I further leave to Sara any love that I may have had left inside of me when I died, as well as many of the things that we did not do together, the places that we did not go together, and the things that I did not say to her even though I thought them inside my head.

Jonathon Bender (b.1967–d.1999)

Acknowledgments

A lot of different people helped with this book in a lot of different ways. So thank you Erin Hardin, Susan Nolan, Vladimir Maletic, Ina Kimball, and Kristine Siemieniak for help with different aspects of the research involved in writing this novel. Thank you Sam Lipsyte, Leigh Newman, Donna Heiland, Jessica Anya Blau, Ron Tanner, Geoffrey Becker, and Will Eno for reading different versions of the manuscript. Many thanks go out to the editors of *Post Road*, *New York Tyrant*, *Anemone Sidecar*, *Failbetter*, *Avatar Review*, *JMWW*, *Listen Up*, *Keyhole, The Quarterly*, and *Baltimore Is Reads: An Outdoor Journal* for publishing different parts of *Dear Everybody* over the years. One surprise thank you each goes to Stephen King and to Dave Eggers for their unexpected appreciation of some of the selected letters. Great thanks go to The Tyrant for my time at the castelletto in Sezze where this novel took its final form. More thanks go to Alessandro Gallenzi and Elisabetta Minervini for believing in this novel. A continual thank you goes to Bruce Hunter for his unwavering support. And every other thank you goes to Tita Chico for everything and everything else.